Women of a Certain Age

A Collection of Stories and Poems
accompanied with sketches

By Les Benson

Edited by Patricia Main BA(Hons) MA

(c) Les Benson 2022

Independently published 2022

To my Soulmate Fleur and Family

About the Author - Les Benson

Born 1942 in a small hamlet near Sudbury, Suffolk, where I grew up until the age of ten, I then moved to Colchester Essex where, after schooling, I served an apprenticeship in motor engineering.

At the age of twenty I embarked on a three-week camping holiday with a school mate where we drove, touring about three thousand miles around Europe. On our return I could not settle, thinking there was so much more to life; within six weeks I had joined the Merchant Navy to travel the world, which I was lucky enough to do and be paid for the privilege. Following that period, I worked in various places throughout the UK, eventually settling in the West Country. After retiring, had the time to enjoy pursuing my many hobbies.

In 2018 on meeting some friends, I became interested in one lady who had done some amateur writing; a lifelong friend of my partner, she had brought out a children's book she had written, but although proofed and after much endeavour had never got published. She had also written a few other short stories. Upon reading them, I was intrigued with her work and what had inspired it. She told me she had belonged to a writers' group in Bristol. Following that meeting I decided to have a go at writing myself and was surprised at what followed. I had written a couple of songs in the past when messing around learning to play guitar, but nothing in the way of stories. This was also a personal surprise to me as English had been my worst subject at school! Writing down what was in my head was a steep learning curve and I must admit I've still a long way to go, learning every day. I not only found it interesting but also fascinating how you could create characters, then go on a journey with them into their lives, and being able to relate to their different personalities. This work has evolved over the last five years and turned into a project which I never really envisaged or imagined: that this new hobby would result in me publishing my work.

The collection of writing in this book has come from inside my head. You could say: *why bother to write them down*? That is a question I truthfully cannot answer. I just feel I must, likening the process to an artist painting an abstract composition. In those twilight times when the mind floats between dream and waking, words flow around and around in my head. If I'm not too lazy I catch them and write them down, if not they are lost - though luckily some survive.

Foreword

This book, Women of a Certain Age, was first inspired by a fellow artist's exhibition of portrait paintings of women in their mature years. Seeing them on display made me wonder what type of past lives they might have led, and their status in society. So evolved eight fictitious characters with their individual stories, each of which is faced with decisions, dilemmas and revelations which shaped part of their lives.

There are no complete conclusions. The reader is left to ponder the outcome and decide what they would do faced with the same circumstances.

The other stories and poems have been inspired or prompted by various events, memories, ideas or imagination that came to me from somewhere out there. I even wonder if my uncle Monty, who I'm told was a literary scholar and worked as a Librarian at the British Museum, has been whispering in my ear!

Contents

A Happy New Year to You All

Here we are again
Is it really true
A full twelve months to play with
What are you going to do

Plans might be in the offing
Goals now to achieve
Are you really going to stick to
Only you can believe

Old Father Time still with us
Resolutions by the score
Are you going to make the effort
And fix that squeaky door

Keep intending to get things done
You know you will quite soon
But other things are much more fun
Like a chance to fly to the Moon

Do we have to go on achieving
Making things a better lot
I suppose it's in our nature
To help those who time forgot

I Wish

With my eyes closed while I blow out my birthday candles

I wish I'd been a rock and roll star
To stand on the stage thrashing a guitar
With deafening screams from adoring fans
To be in the hit parade as one of the top bands

On tour I'd be with a group living rough
With late night parties and all that stuff
To perform country wide and loving it all
Like a band of marauders, our life's just a ball

Writing great songs, with music that fits to the beat
With a rhythm that you can't help tapping your feet
Strobes light the stage, as the crowd scream and shout
All those great amps stacked, banging the sound out

Dream of those days of Oh Boy and Top of the Pops
It seemed that time of rock and roll never stopped
With that sound in my ears, I can't help myself move
Rock and roll was my teens but I'm still in the groove

That wish is a dream that sometime floats in my head
Sadly though now a lot of my rock idols are dead
The old songs still covered, played with adds on TV
This rock and roll lives on, now part of our history

Life's Mementoes

It was one of those mid-winter days when the weather outside was dry but bitterly cold. I had arrived early at the Salvation Army Citadel in Bath for the Writing Group meeting which I enjoy attending when time allows. I was sitting at a table having a cup of tea while waiting in the Sally Ann cafe, which at the time was about two thirds full, contributing to the windows becoming partially steamed up with condensation.

My attention was drawn to a lady sat with two large carrier bags also having a hot drink, no doubt, like many other of the customers, she had come in here to have some form of warm sustenance to get respite against the cold outside. She was sat in the corner with a view towards the windows, the natural light highlighting her face, which was elderly and lined with bright blue watery eyes. I noted her wrinkled hands and the band of gold she wore on her wedding finger.

What struck me most was her attire with a dark blue scarf wound around her greying hair adorned with a small sunflower. Her chequered patterned topcoat was the worse for wear, frayed on the collar and cuffs. In my mind she may have been sleeping rough? But what most intrigued me was the adornments she had pinned to the front of her coat. First, was a memorial poppy which I thought unusual being it was January, also a white hart highland brooch and a pink rose, along with a small silvery bell and heart that caught the light. I wondered … were these trinkets her treasured mementoes?

I like painting portraiture so could not resist the urge; I took out my small drawing pad and proceeded to sketch her portrait, which luckily only took a short while as I was prompted by another Writing Group member that we should proceed upstairs to our meeting. I would really have liked to have spoken to her, but I don't know if I'd have had the cheek.

Sometime later I was looking at my sketch of this elderly lady and felt inspired to paint her portrait. Her character had fascinated me back at the cafe but now as I started to paint the picture her face looked collected and calm as my imagination started to take over. I wondered who she might be, sat there; her expression was as if pondering, maybe the memories of another time or place, or recalling happenings in her past life. I thought perhaps she had fallen on hard times and done so through her own doing, or was it the fault of others causing the misfortunes befallen to her? That thin gold band indicating being married, made me ponder affairs of the heart - was there a partner somewhere? But my fascination was once again drawn to her mementoes pinned to her coat? Did they represent a record of past events in life? The poppy of remembrance - was it of a loved one lost? The white hart brooch - did it signify a Scottish connection? Perhaps the silver bell was from a wedding. The shinning heart a christening, or the pink rose faded from its original red, was it a Valentine token given in love?

When looking at the finished portrait of this solitary sitting figure with her worn attire and ageing face, with her set gaze lost in thought, adorned with these medals of her life, with this almost symbolic cup and saucer on the table in front of her it brought to mind the words of the song *Streets of London*. The ballad describes the lifestyle of people who had fallen on hard times going about their everyday mundane existence in contrast to people going about their daily business in relative comfort with trivial moans and groans who don't always relate or see the reality in the suffering of others worse off.

I often think of that lady and wonder where she may be and how she is managing her life? Since Covid, our Writing Group has resumed and I have enquired about her at the cafe, showing the staff a photo of the painting on my phone, but no one remembers her or knows of her. Most likely all my suppositions are completely wrong and she is quite contented with her lot. Whoever or wherever she may be, I wish her well.

Tell Me That Story

Daddy!
Tell me that story
That you told to me
That when you were younger
You lived in a tree.

Oh, tell me that story
When they called you the ape man
And you swung through the trees
And your name was Tarzan.

Tell me that story
Now you're old and grey
About your friend Jane
Who turned out to be gay.

Oh, tell me that story
How it used to be
When you fell in love with a monkey
And my mum was a chimpanzee

Sally

Lost Horizons

As in the words of the song: *One of these mornings, you're going to rise up singing, you're going to spread your wings, and take to the sky.*

The morning sun was just peeping over the distant hills as it does these spring mornings at this early hour, little by little the light penetrates down through the dales, creeping along the stone walls toward the farmhouse, bringing a warmth to the grey stone.

Sally was up, looking out the window; further down the valley the Jacobs' farmhouse lights were on as always in the early morning. Standing in her dressing gown she pondered, wondering which far off lands this rising sun had been shining on while she had been asleep, which exotic country so different from hers. This country, this county of Yorkshire, this place where she had spent all of her life - born and bred into this rural farming community – here, where farming is a way of life, not just a nine to five job.

What were these feelings of restlessness she had been getting? For some time now they had been building up inside her; was it through reading too many travel books? watching too many documentaries seeing how people lived in other countries? taking an interest in seeing what it was like the other side of the world? These inner feelings for a sense of adventure … was this her mid-life crisis?

Her train of thought was broken by the sound of the toilet flush across the landing. Brian was already up, finishing his ablutions, so she now made haste; they'd both be outdoors soon enough. Hearing their son Jamie's 4 x 4 pull into the yard setting the dogs barking, she washed and dressed quickly before going downstairs, then just a quick cuppa, breakfast later as there was work to be done.

The spring lambing was finished now, an endurance of all-night vigils, as all other years as long as she could remember. Although vital to their livelihood, it had never lost its fascination and had also been a wonderful way to introduce the children to the facts of life. Now there was stock to feed and maintain and markets to prepare for, jobs to sort in the fields. There was very little let-up getting the flock outside with dipping and shearing soon upon them.

This terrain could be a hard life to work especially in winter months, fighting against the elements: cutting winds, whipping rain, wading through the snow waist-high looking for buried sheep. It is certainly a different picture from that seen by visitors in its idealistic setting during the summer months, when they remark how it looks like paradise with fields lush and green in the sunshine.

The seasons come and go with a certain regularity, some harsher; some kinder. Right now, the swallows have arrived from spreading their wings in far off Africa, flying *all* that way to breed and return, maintaining this ritual, their natural instincts of migration over the centuries. Nothing like her own self-imposed lifestyle set in one place in this world, only now realising the repetition of all those past years of her life. The doubt about her own future had built over the last couple of years, with the thought of the rest of her life lacking a self-experience outside of this county, outside this country, even this continent. She had fulfilled her commitment to her marriage … to her family.

Looking back, she had been contented, more than contented, she had been happy in love with her life, her husband and raising her children. It was only lately that she had looked at herself as an individual, realising she was becoming a mirror image of her mother; a woman who had not travelled far, had never flown in an aeroplane. It all seemed so predictable. Geography had always been one of her favourite lessons during her schooldays. Knowing there was a whole world out there and you only have one life, it's not a rehearsal.

To Sally it had all started to seemed the same; everybody knew her and she knew everybody. She longed to meet people from other walks of life, to be able to discuss things other than farming, not continually talking about problems arising from the weather or how government policies are affecting the price of commodities.

Sally had been married to Brian some thirty-five years, their two children now adults. She had no regrets on how her children had grown up in wide, open spaces of the farmland and fresh air to give them a healthy start to life and their good education, which had carried them through agricultural college. Both enjoying their countryside lifestyle.

She had known Brian from her schooldays, him being two years older, subsequently on a personal level getting acquainted at community gatherings, shows and local fairs.

Jamie the elder child had finished farming college and now returned home, eventually settling down with his girlfriend in a small cottage not far from them. He was progressive, with all his up-to-date knowledge and practices along with his own ideas; his father was pleased at his interest and enthusiasm but sometimes had reservation with some of them.

Pam, their daughter, had seen some of the world travelling during her gap year, enjoying the whole experience, but even she had returned, settling down with a local farming family. She still helped out part-time on their farm, organising the stock, marketing, and accounts. It was still very much a family affair.

Brian had noticed for some time now Sally would stop and be lost in a dream-like state, at first he used to say, *penny for your thoughts*, and she used to laugh it off saying: 'Oh nothing,' with a shrug. But lately he had started to worry about these reoccurrences when she seemed completely lost in thought.

One night, both lying in bed, Brian's concerns prompted him to say something.

'What's the matter, Sal. You seem to be away with the fairies. I just feel there something wrong with you, or us?'

'I just feel I need a break.'

'A break from what?'

'Everything.'

'What? You mean a holiday?'

'It's not that … I mean a proper break'

'Well, you know we couldn't leave the farm for too long.' Brian trying appease, 'but I'm sure Jamie could cope. You mean like a couple or three weeks away?' He was clearly trying to sound enthusiastic. 'What do you want to do? Go on a cruise, maybe one of those river cruises? We could sell that small top field to Jack if he is still interested.' He was wanting to please her. 'I'm sure we could sort something.'

Brian felt he was clutching at straws.

'No, it's not that. You still don't understand.' She said helplessly.

'Well, *you* tell me then, help me understand.' He let out a sigh of bewilderment.

Sally took a deep breath. 'Brian, I love you dearly but … but I'm not happy with my life.'

'Oh, come on, we have a laugh and we no-way argue like we used to … and money's not so tight now.' He was trying to humour her.

'It's not like that.' she hesitated, 'I need to go away on my own for a while.'

Silence.

Brian now realised something was drastically wrong. He turned and kissed her. 'Please don't do this to me … I *know* I'm not perfect, is it me? What? What?'

'It's *not your fault* at all. It's me.' She said, trying to explain. 'Brian, we married when I was only twenty and at the time it meant everything to me. I wanted so much for us to be together … to have a family and work the farm. I've loved all these years. I have no regrets, honestly. It's just that I can't go on like this. I'm scared that I will suffer a mental breakdown.'

Brian wrapped his arms around her, thinking to himself that he'd call the doctor tomorrow. They must have someone, a counsellor who could give some advice and would be able to talk with her.

'Look let's sleep on all this. I'm sure we can work it out. Please let me try to understand. Please, Please! Let's sleep on it.' He murmured. 'I promise you we'll talk about it in the morning.' He leant over and kissed her again, then, lying close together eventually they fell asleep.

The vet was with them early the next morning, by lunch time he had left. But despite the ordinariness, it was obvious that late night conversation had been on Brian's mind; he'd been thinking how best to approach the subject. All the family were at the table for lunch - he had made sure their two children were at lunch. Once everyone was seated, Brian started to speak.

'I wanted us all together because I want you to hear this.' Brian took a deep breath. 'Look, Mum's saying she needs a break from all of this, here on the farm.'

Both Jamie and Pam looked quizzically at him.

Sally felt it might be better if she said something. 'It's like this,' starting to explain. 'I just want time on my own … in different surroundings.'

Brian was listening, but still shaking his head in disbelief, 'What about me and what about the children?' he asked, searching for a reason.

'Brian, they are both adults, they have their own lives to lead,' she was still trying her best to explain,' looking at both the children. 'I'm not saying I want to go away forever. I just need a break, travel a bit, have some time to myself.'

'You've been reading too many of those bloody travel books.' Brian said, resentment colouring his voice.

'Brian,' she was really trying to make a point. 'Next birthday I'll be fifty-six. I've never been anywhere. Yes, I know we've had the odd times away and they have been lovely, it's not that. I can't just live here like this until I die.'

'Mum,' said Pam 'What's brought all this on?'

'Don't you ever feel there is more to life than just living here, that your brain needs to think about something other than farming.' she said, hoping to make a connection on how she felt.

'Sally,' Brian sounding a bit more reasonable. 'Everyone has fantasies … owning a second home by the sea, having the most up to date car or truck, living an uncomplicated life with plenty of money in the bank. Everyone window shops, but accepts the fact you can't have what you can't afford. Most people realise that and make the most of it. Everyone thinks *the grass is greener on the other side,* and you know as well as I do it's not always the case.' Trying to convince her, make her see reason.

'Darling, people change, sometimes you find out that you're living a lie to yourself.'

'Well, I never saw this coming! So what you're saying is, without a care in the world you want to bugger off and leave us all?' Brian's temper flared.

'Well, okay! Yes, if you want to put it like that.'

'God! So you want a separation?' By now Brian had stood up, becoming flustered

'It's not like that at all,' She protested, trying to find the right words. 'I just need to find myself.'

'You have really *lost* me now!'

'Sally, now inhaled deeply, she was determined to get through to them. 'Brian,' (she felt she had to really spell it out.) 'You haven't been listening to *me*, this is not about money or material things it is about what goes on in my head. Self-fulfilment - my acceptance of whom I am, being true to myself. I need to stop pretending everything is all right, when it's not.'

Brian looked across at her still not convinced he knew what she was talking about. He could see her welling up, realising the determination in her voice. He did not want to lose her and wanted her to be happy.

She reassured them that keeping in touch would be no problem with the internet, email, Zoom and mobile phone.

Although there were many more conversations on the subject, the family began to accept the inevitability of the situation though at times the atmosphere was strained, with the workload being heavy through the following weeks, and everybody sharing in with the jobs to be done.

During this time, Sally obtained her passport and planned where she would start her journey, studying the maps in her atlas, reading up on the different cultures. By the end of the summer, she had a visa and arranged a posting to work at an orphanage in Honduras, something which her local church was involved with as a sponsored charity. This was just the chance she wanted. With this all set up, Brian had become more understanding. He felt respect for what she was doing, but still resented her going. For her the dream was becoming reality. She knew that her journal would be a record completely different from anything she had done before, opening her eyes to unfamiliar surroundings. The feeling of excitement was mounting within her, something which she had never experienced before. She was pleased that, in the end, Brian had conceded to her wishes and realised she was on a mission. She told herself (and him) that it would only be for twelve months but she knew in her heart that was not the truth; she would have to see where her new life would take her.

The day came. The taxi arrived. She stood motionless at their front-room window as so many times in the past with the landscape stretched out down the dales before her. This time, though, her thoughts were in conflict. Turning towards the front door, she was determined not to cry. It wasn't selfishness; it was all about being true to herself. This was not like the stress they had endured in the past: disasters that had struck their livelihood, that had also affected others in their farming community, accounting for farmers going bust and some eventually even committing suicide.

Over the years, all these things had happened and they had managed to pull through it all as a family. This, now, was purely about her life; her mental state that wanted and needed to be satisfied. She edged her way out of the front doorway towards Brian and the two children along with the dogs who stood by the front gate. They had left Sally with time to herself to say goodbye to the house.

Brian was still bewildered, disappointed that he had been unable to dissuade her and, although with reluctance, he had in the end accepted her decision. He had already handed her modest sized case to the taxi driver who was now waiting with the passenger door open. The farewell hugs and kisses - brief although given through an atmosphere of resentment – left her with mixed emotions.

Seated in the taxi, waving goodbye, she was off. Her eyes by now damp with tears but knowing she *had* to do this. From now on every day was going to be a new experience for her. She had set her route to her first destination but who knows how it will all work out. Excitement again was starting to grow inside her as she thought of the small journal in her luggage and how she would record her travel experiences in it each day. Perhaps one day, maybe when the children or grandchildren read them, they will gain some understanding as to why she had gone away on her own to find herself. She hoped her journal writings would reflect that there was no malice in her leaving and how desires needed to be fulfilled. Travelling towards the airport, she viewed the surrounding Yorkshire countryside spread out, so familiar that she felt she had never really fully appreciated it being there; after all, she had known nothing else.

Arriving at the airport she felt confident and was quite pleased with herself managing to find her way through to the South American Airways flight desk. Standing at check-in queue, there were few Europeans among the passengers. She overheard incomprehensible conversations in foreign tongues and realised that she was in for a culture shock. All about the waiting lounge there was the hustle and bustle of passengers, people of different ethnic groups from other nations of the world all on a journey somewhere in their lives. To her this was so new, interesting and so enlightening. Her journey had properly begun. Sally now sat having a coffee with her flight-bag beside her feet trying to relax but there was so much unfamiliar activity going on, she couldn't help people watching. Then over the loud speaker came the announcement of her flight number, destination and boarding gate. Taking in the information, she readied herself to move, just then, her mobile phone rang; it was Pam. She must be phoning a last farewell, she thought with a smile.

'Hello darling, just having a coffee. They have just announced boarding, so I can't talk long.'

'Mum! It's Dad he's had an accident. The ambulance has just taken him to hospital.' Sally could hear the panic in her voice.

'What's happened?' Sally, desperate to know.

'He was up in the top field on the quad-bike and it toppled over on him. They think he has fractured his leg. They've taken him to St. Andrews.'

'Shall I go straight to the Hospital?' Sally asked without hesitation, then inquiring 'Where is Jamie?'

'Mum, Jamie's with dad. He followed the ambulance.'

'Was he conscious when they put him in the ambulance?' asked Sally.

'Yes, just in a lot of pain. Mum what are you going to do?'

The address system was again announcing boarding for her flight.

'Leave it with me I'll work something out, everything will be all right. I must go now darling, bye.'

Was it her inbuilt sense of duty as a wife or a strong deep-down love of Brian ... this man who had been such a big part of her life. All the past and present was racing through her brain trying to reconcile all the information. She must do the right thing. In time, there's every chance Brian will mend and be back to normal in no time, and then ... will time stand still for her? Should she wait for another day ... or was it all for nothing. Was she strong enough or was it an opportunity lost?

Over the address system came an announcement: last call for boarding her flight.

Her love for Brian and their children had not changed, but her love of life had. Did she really have any control over her future life? Without another thought, Sally put away her mobile and then stood, picked up her flight-bag and started walking. The one thing she had no control of was the way tears were filling her eyes.

Never throw your dreams away
Keep them for another day
For fortune shines on those who persist
Regret is the reward for opportunities missed
So, stand by them with drive and ambition
Then your dreams will come to fruition
Always have that possibility to renew
Maybe someday they will come true

Spring : A Time to Cherish

The land lies dormant for time to build its resources
Moving nature's gestation process to take its courses
Temperatures rise combined with showers fall
Signals pulse throughout with spontaneous call
Prompts the spring season it's time to start
There's no holding back this throbbing heart

Bursting, budding, as seeds break their shell
As the earth reacts to each germinating cell
Pushing and probing as roots search out their nutrition
Later their process of production will reach fruition
Trees and foliage their canopies now turning green
Adorned with blossoms giving an early floral scene

All manner of insects busy with pheromonal release
While others flit amongst the blooms on a nectar feast
An awakening stretch for those who've hibernated
This animal kingdom urges to breed and be mated
Birds sing, heralding in the time with soaring song
Some arrive from distant lands after travelling long

Building nests and dens to raise crying-out young
Tending eggs, infants' wants, frantic feeding begun
Upon this our earth needs for all of life to flourish
Our sun and rain give all living things to nourish
Longer daylight hours of time a sense to growing
duty
As nature works relentlessly towards achieving its
beauty

This is springtime which brings thoughts of promise

A chance to clear-out, renew ourselves to be honest
Time to watch and listen, observe nature at its best
Accept its part, to relate, preserve, nurture and invest
Appreciate this world, it's shared destiny; we all
belong
With open eyes we should all realise, where we are
going wrong

Love at First Flight

Spring had come early this year to Keynsham Park, the sun was shining and the flowers beds were coming into bloom. A wonderful array of large, shady, mature trees set within the great expanse of green grass carpet sloping down towards the river. Along its banks, numerous groups of lovely slender trees and bushes, all budding out in leaf, the feeling of nature bursting into life.

It was only yesterday I had arrived in the area, having flown in from North Africa, a long flight, and I was still feeling tired. Now, the middle of the day, taking a look around, I was feeling peckish and looking to have something to eat. I went over to one of the tables at the café and, just as I was looking to see what food was available, I looked up and couldn't believe my eyes - there she was eating on another table, I recognised her straight away.

I don't think she had noticed me before, but I remember her, she was with us during the flight. Fancy that, her coming and settling in the same area, and at the same place as me. As I was looking over at her, she lifted her head, and looked straight at me. I could feel my heart jump. 'Isn't she lovely!' I thought. I imagined we must be about the same age and could easily tell by her features that we were from the same place. I also guessed she had come all this way for the same reasons as myself, as our past generations had: to have a better chance in life.

I thought she looked just perfect with those wonderful eyes. I could tell the way she held her gaze at me and tilted her head to one side, that she didn't mind me looking at her. I was just thinking of going over to her, when suddenly there was a noise from behind me causing me to look away quickly; when I turned back, she had gone. I looked around but she was nowhere to be seen. The park had become quite crowded by now, everyone enjoying the good weather, so it was a job to see if she was still about.

All the rest of the day I was so happy I couldn't stop singing to myself thinking about her, even that night I was still wondering what she may be doing. I had been fortunate to find a place to sleep in the area, only a short distance from the park.

The next day I arrived early at the park; the sky looked a bit cloudy but it was still warm. I was hoping she might be there again. As the morning passed, I took my time having a good look around. I went down by the river where there were some people walking with dogs, and others with children; all kinds of wild life were about. The sun was now starting to break through the clouds and rising higher in the sky; the day was moving on. I was starting to feel down … perhaps she won't come to the park again. Was it just me getting all romantic? We hadn't even met properly.

As I came back up over the grassy slope, I caught my breath, 'Yes!' She was there at the top of the park on one of the benches. She looked as beautiful as ever and she could see me coming. I called to her in our native tongue and she called back to me. Oh, what a lovely voice she had! Like a flash I was beside her. At first, she moved along a bit away from me, I could gather she was a little shy. Then I moved close to her again and I couldn't believe it, she just stayed there she didn't move away or reject me. Is this really happening to me? My heart was racing, and my voice seemed to have gone as I remembered all those things I had thought about the night before when my mind had been rambling, imagining us being together as mates, even building a home and having a family. It just seemed right somehow. Fate, nature, call it what you like, had brought us together. Just there looking at each other, not a sound past between us; she nudged closer and I could feel her warmth. As the time passed, we gradually started communicating in our language. We just couldn't stop. We had so much in common. It was from then on, I knew we would be as one, just there together, lost in our love.

Spring was definitely in the air; a warm light breeze blew up across the park ruffling us. Knowingly we looked at each other, our thoughts as one. Hopping down from the bench, we each picked up a few pieces of thin, dry twig in our beaks then, taking flight up into the sky, we flew towards the woodlands down by the river

It was Love At First Flight.

Green Park Station

Enter this sky lit Cathedral place
Sounds of music now fill this space
I look around its structure built to last
All I see, a sad reflection of its past

Once a building of grandeur purpose fit
Now left a mishmash of kiosk or cafe to sit
Open spaces left as dumping ground
Where occasional market can be found

Just sit, Reflect awhile
Close your eyes, let the mind glide
As your imagination takes ride
Can you smell that smell of sooty smoke
What scene before you will it evoke

A whistle blast, a gush of steam, the senses contrive
Crowded voices, hustle bustle brings the scene alive
People in action, trolleys rattle, cases pass to and fro
Some meeting greeting, and others hurrying to go

A mighty engine hauls approaching train
Its exuberance of power releases the strain
As screeching brakes applied, slowing to halt
Hitting buffers stops final motion, with a jolt

Sound address system, alerts attention calls out
Voiced announcement inaudible, creates doubt
Time of trains, pending arrivals, giving out
information
The train now leaving platform two for its destination

Faces of joy, long awaited arrivals receiving
Faces of sorrow, of heartache, with tears of leaving
Farewells, goodbyes to relations, lovers, friends
Some departing never to return to these ends

A chuff-in funnel signals steams up time to go
Jarring medley as slamming carriage doors give echo
Trusted guard his whistle blown, Green flag waved
Railways ingenious signal play of time and effort
saved

How many passengers trod these worn stone floors
City business, seaside treats, and soldiers off to wars
A plethora of stories played out upon platforms here
As the driver moves the power of steam into gear

Smoke belches forth filling cavernous domes
The mighty engine train starts to strain from zone
Piston push on giant wheels turn with mighty force
Moving, creaking, sets steel on steel to hold the
course

Gone from here those days of yesteryears travel
When passengers had time-tables to unravel
A mode of transport provided for rich and poor
Once functioned from this place, but no more

Brunel his engineering endeavours still reign
Sliced across East To West this country's terrain
Its noble history acted out within these vaulted halls
Never to return those times past, as progress calls

June 2021

Gabriella

Model Choice

Gabriella stood in front of the mirror putting the finishing touches to her apparel, half smiling at her reflection, she thought: not bad for a woman in her sixties. She still had a fine elegant look which had followed her from those modelling days. Her posture was upright, her face having clear smooth skin, apart from a few lines that come with age. She had always taken care of her appearance. High cheek bones still made her attractive, with eyes that still sparkled. Here was a woman with a regular routine, hairdressers, massage, exercise with personal trainer and more. A woman who had never known manual work, never known what it was like to get down on hands and knees to clean. Pushing her shoulder length hair up, she clasped her necklace tog, she was ready.

The apartment in Park Lane was still part owned by her ex-husband who had no intention of selling. In fact, it was part of the divorce settlement, which allowed her to reside until her demise and also came with a generous lump sum payment and alimony.

She had her regrets about the divorce, just over two years ago. Those memories of their times together before the boys were born. Travelling the world with her modelling career. As time had passed, they had both had their flings, but nothing serious enough to upset their marriage. It wasn't until Lloyd had been promoted, which meant spending long periods of time abroad with the foreign office, that it all started to go wrong.

He was now married to a woman twenty-three years his junior, an interpreter at the Embassy while he was away working in Miyaland.

Their boys now grown up, one living in Scotland with his male partner, and one in Canada and married, both him and his wife very career minded. There were no grandchildren on the horizon. The boys were both very considerate, always in contact and inviting her to visit, whenever she had the time. Money was never a problem, so she always made the effort to see them.

She previously owned a car but now found it an inconvenience so taxied everywhere it was so easy from where she lived.

Afternoon tea at the Ritz was a regular monthly occurrence with her two close friends. They had been so supportive over the initial divorce shock, her having to accept that it was for real. He wanted a complete break and was not coming back to her.

Also in her life was Henry, who had been a long-time friend of her and her husband. A lovely man, wonderful company, someone to go to the theatre or out to dinner with, and no advances towards her after being out together. He was an art dealer in his seventies, and one of the old school, who did not advertise his sexuality. It was never discussed, just a confidence between them.

As she alighted from the taxi it was about three in the afternoon. Walking up toward the Ritz's main entrance, the doorman opening the door with a pleasant "good afternoon, Madame". She nodded, smiled and walked in. Straight away she saw the familiar face of Angela.

"Hello darling how are you, is Gloria here yet." stepping forward and kissing her cheek.

"Oh yes, she's just powdering her nose."

They walked slowly towards the tea rooms, within less than a minute Gloria was by their side.

"Hello, how are you, Gabriella, how are those boys of yours doing?"

"Absolutely fine, Darren wants me to go over to Canada for Christmas, which would be rather nice."

By now they were seated, and had ordered. The tearoom's decor was sumptuous, with its high-class atmosphere. All three ladies sat calm, collected, relaxed, dressed in their finery. This was a lifestyle they were accustomed to. It was a chance to catch up on the latest gossip. It was something they looked forward to.

Well into the afternoon tea, Gabriella couldn't

help noticing the middle-aged man sitting at the table adjacent. She noticed on occasions he would look away from his company to glance, she thought, in her direction. She also noticed he was an attractive man for his age.

Time passed, and while Gloria was settling up, as it was her treat this time, Angela and Gabriella walked through, out into the foyer.

Angela turned to her and said in a low serious voice. "I didn't say anything while we were at the table, but I read in the paper this morning that there has been a coup against the government in Miyaland; isn't that where Lloyd is attached to the Embassy? I hope you don't mind my mentioning it, it's just that I felt I ought to."

"Thank you, Angela, I'm sure he'll be alright they always get special protection."

Angela then made her excuses and went off to the cloakroom.

Standing there alone Gabriella saw the man who had been sitting at the adjacent table, walking towards her.

"Hello, my name is Christopher Parffet, please excuse me, I know we haven't been introduced, but I couldn't help noticing you. If I'm not mistaken, you're Gabriella Gordon?"

"That is correct; how did you recognise me?" she answered with some pleasure.

"I'm a photographer, doing some fashion shoots for the Koron agency. I've noticed your face displayed in their hallway of fame photos, as one of their past icons of the trade."

"Really! I never realised I was an icon" she lightly laughed.

Just then Gloria and Angela walked past,

saying in unison: "Bye, see you next month." Smiling with knowingly raised eyebrows.

"Bye" said Gabriella, looking at their expressions as they walked away, knowing full well what they were surmising. She turned back to face Christopher. "There go the terrible twins!" she exclaimed.

He smiled, then said, "I don't know if you would be interested but, I heard it mentioned at Koron the other day that they were looking to sign some mature female models for some of their shoots. They have already signed Veronica Richardson. No doubt you remember her from the seventies. Anyway, I'll give you my card, just in case you might like me to mention you to them."

"Thank you … err," as she looked at the card, "… Christopher, that is very good of you, it's been nice meeting you."

"My pleasure" he said with a broad smile. "Hope to see you again."

"Yes, thanks again, I'll have a think about it, goodbye." she said, as she walked away toward the main doorway.

Exiting out into the sunshine, she felt there was still a warmth in the air.

The doorman hailed the black cab forward. Thanking him as she made her way towards the taxi, then getting in, she felt happy with herself, even a bit smug that *he* should have recognised her.

The journey proceeded through the traffic, towards Park Lane with its usual congestion. After a while, the cab turned on to the road that ran parallel to the park, deciding to walk she asked the cabby to pull over: "Please could you stop here?"

"Ok madam." retorted the cabby, following

her request, manoeuvring the vehicle to a halt by the side of the pavement. Paying the cabby, she then turned to cross the road via the crossing, a few steps along from where she was standing.

It was still a clear bright late afternoon, walking along towards home which was not that far. She looked through the railings into the park seeing the children playing, some of the young ones obviously in the care of grandparents. Something, she was yet to experience, or if ever, as it looked at present in her future.

There was such a lovely feeling in the air, here she was fancy free. Her thoughts inevitably turned to her meeting with Christopher. Feeling herself take a pose, as she walked with one foot directly in front of the other as though she was on the catwalk again. Yes, she could do it, she still had that about her, that sense of glamour in the industry that she missed. No ties in her personal life, this could be a new beginning, her life could have a purpose again. She had the busy schedule of her self-indulgent life, but nothing to fire her imagination at present. Taking on this challenge would stimulate her in a new way. Remembering when she was a model it was hard work. Would she be able to cope at her age? Why look on the negative side, her personal trainer had remarked how good she was at her fitness regime he had set her.

That's it, she had made her decision, she would contact Christopher tomorrow morning.

Later that evening after her meal she settled on the sofa with a coffee, she switched on the television for the evening news. Following a couple of home affairs items, her attention was caught by the report coming in from Lirvob the capital of Miyaland, the on-the-ground reporter pictured dressed in blue helmet and flak jacket. He was reporting that the situation had worsened. There had been conflicting reports coming in of killings and kidnappings, some of civilians who were associated with the British Government had been targeted. This was believed to be due to the association of British money that had been propping up the regime. "The situation in Lirvob is stable at present, and a night time curfew in place controlled by the state guard." The news now moved on to another item.

She felt disturbed, by what she had seen, concerned for Lloyd's well-being. She thought she would phone the Embassy tomorrow, and try and speak to an acquaintance of her ex-husband. The news concluded, followed by the weather forecast of a bright outlook for London. Sitting back on the sofa, putting her feet up, she now resolved herself to watching the evening's entertainment.

Rising quite early the next day, she breakfasted and tidied around before the home help arrived. After showering she dressed for the morning. She would be off to her personal trainer by ten o'clock, she looked in the mirror at the finished job in her sport-gym attire. Yes, I must phone that Christopher chap this morning she thought, I will take a stab at it, they can only say yes or no.

After her morning gym session, she arrived back at the apartment. While showering she recalled earlier telling her personal trainer of her encounter with the fashion photographer, and the prospect of an offer of modelling. Straight away he had said "go for it, why not?". This had given her confidence a boost.

Out of the shower and dressed, she now phoned Christopher but, getting his answer phone, she left a message, saying she would be happy for him to put her name forward, leaving her phone number in case Koron wished to contact her. Now she would make that phone call to the Embassy.

Phoning the British Embassy, she eventually managed to get through to the right department to speak to Brian Bradshaw. He was sympathetic of her concerns regarding Lloyd and the situation in Miyaland.

"The problem is," said Brian "we are still getting conflicting reports as to what's happening on the ground. The Embassy in Lirvob is saying and I must stress this is unofficial, that they may start evacuating staff soon if the situation becomes worse. I'm sorry to be so vague about the whole thing, but let me have your phone number, then if I get any more information, I'll let you know."

Gabriella thanked him, said goodbye, then put the receiver down.

No sooner had she done so than the internal phone rang to inform her that Henry was waiting downstairs. Putting down the receiver, she was ready to meet Henry for lunch, then off to the art gallery preview, which she had been looking forward to. It was one of her favourite artists, Hannah Roberts; already one of her works hung in Gabriella's hallway. She had bought the painting because she liked it, on Henry's advice. The artist had become a rising star in the art world though she was now in her late fifties.

She grabbed her coat, came out her apartment, then proceeded down the staircase. As she descended towards the foyer she could see Henry standing there waiting. A smart man, impeccably dressed in a made-to-measure suit, tall with thinning grey hair.

"Hallo, my dear, lovely to see you, you look wonderful." said Henry, spoken in eloquent tone. "I have the taxi waiting for us."

Now on their way to the restaurant for lunch, she felt her anxiety subside.

It was comforting to be out with Henry. He was fully aware of her concerns, sympathising with her regarding to Lloyd. She told him she had been in touch with the Embassy. The conversation then changed to chatting about the exhibition. Henry mentioned about her previous purchase and how the value would go up, as Hannah Roberts makes her mark in the art world.

They were both seated now at the restaurant table. After their menu choice, Gabriella mentioned the chance meeting with the photographer chap at the Ritz earlier in the week, and how he had recommended she have another go at modelling.

"What a wonderful idea, I think it would be good for you. Sometimes one needs to get out there and meet some new people." Henry enthused. "Away from your set of friends, and old fuddy duddies like me. If you don't mind me saying."

They finished their meal and then proceeded to walk to the Bellom Gallery, which was only a short distance away. Conscious now, as she was walking with Henry, of how smart he was, she straightened her posture. She was on the catwalk again.

It was a lovely way to spend the afternoon browsing the gallery, pleased with her previous purchase. Looking at the art works on show, and their asking price, *her* painting looked to being a good investment. As she wandered around with Henry, he eventually introduced her to an associate along with the artist herself, a slimish bohemian type with tasselled hair. Later, Henry wandered off with his acquaintance, leaving Gabriella talking to Hannah. She told her of buying one of her art works from an exhibition at Brighton some two years ago, saying she had bought the painting because she really liked it. After more small talk, Hannah said she had enjoyed speaking to her, as this was not really her scene, and although she felt she enjoyed the success, she was much happier home in her own surroundings. Hannah had followed on saying, if ever Gabriella thought of visiting East Anglia it would be nice to see her. They said their goodbyes. Gabriella and Henry then made their way home. He was going to meet a client, so he was dropping her off from the taxi at Park Lane.

When inside her apartment she noticed the answer machine was flashing. She checked the messages; Koron had phoned wondering if she could come for an interview tomorrow afternoon at two o'clock. Could she please phone back to confirm.

That evening on the news the report was from Lirvob airport, featuring the same television correspondent as the previous evening. He was saying that the coup situation had worsened and they were evacuating British nationals. In the background you could make out the crowds of men, women and children with their belongings. They had declared a state of emergency in Miyaland. With deepening concern, she decided she must phone Brian Bradshaw again. On phoning the embassy, she found he was unavailable, so left a message for him.

As she walked through the large glass door of the offices of Koron she saw Christopher sitting in the foyer; he noticed her and rose to his feet.

"Hello, I thought I'd come along and give you some moral support."

"Hello," she replied smiling, "That's very good of you, I didn't think there was anything wrong with my morals that they needed supporting".

Christopher laughed. "You know what I mean. I'll take you up to the offices if you like."

"That's very kind of you, thanks." She answered.

Once at the offices Christopher said he would wait at reception until she came out. The receptionist took her to the interview. There was, she presumed, what was a young model coming out the doorway. Then the receptionist put her head around the door into the room and said Gabriella Gordon had arrived. She then beckoned her to go in saying they are ready to see you.

On entering Gabriella saw three people sitting the other side of the table.

They all rose in unison offering her a greeting. and shaking her hand, inviting her to sit down.

The panel consisted of two females and one male, all three under forty years of age. The interview was conducted in an orderly manner outlining what the job entailed, and the reason they were now taking on more mature female models. As time progressed the interview became less formal, chatting about her past career and what she had done since.

Eventually the session drew to a close. The lady in the centre the Chief Executive, spoke: "We would like to offer you a position with Koron agencies, subject to a shoot. If you *are* interested, please take this contract for your perusal, and by all means take legal advice." She followed saying, "The industry has become a lot more competitive now, so I must emphasize. if you do join us, we will require one hundred percent commitment on your part. I'm sure you will enjoy the challenge. The receptionist will arrange your initial shoot if you speak to her on the way out."

She thanked them and said her goodbyes, as she was walking towards the reception desk, Christopher come forward to meet her.

"How did it go?"

"Fine I think, they want me to have a shoot before they finalise things."

At the reception, she then made arrangements for the shoot.

"Christopher," the receptionist said, "I've booked you in for Gabriella's photo shoot next Thursday morning, is that all right?"

"Fine" said Christopher. "Shall we say six thirty a.m.?"

Gabriella took an intake of breath, Christopher saw her reaction and laughed, "Only kidding, ten am will be fine at my studio." They all smiled and the two of them left the building.

Out in the street Christopher turned to her." How about some lunch?"

After a very pleasant lunch with Christopher, during which she had enjoyed his company, she found she was looking forward to working with him. Confirming the date for next Thursday they said their goodbyes. As she walked away a sense of sheer pleasure came over her.

Returning to her apartment, she put the radio

on, and there was a news bulletin saying that the airport at Lirvob had been sealed off by the insurgent opposition. This meant the evacuation procedure had come to a halt. The city of Lirvob was coming under fire. The British government were holding an emergency meeting on the situation. Just then the phone rang. It was Brian from the embassy.

"Gabriella, I would like to call around to see you. This evening if possible. There have been some developments, and I've got something I need to tell you personally."

"That's fine" she answered "what sort of time?"

"Say five o'clock if convenient."

"Yes, I'll see you then, goodbye".

Later that evening Brian arrived. A man of medium height, wearing a pinstriped suit, just as she remembered him, having met him before at an Embassy function. On his arrival she guided him through to the lounge, and offered him a drink. He said would she mind if he had a whisky, so she poured two. Sitting opposite one another in the lounge, Brian became pensive as he started to explain the situation which had now transpired and was ongoing.

"Yesterday, the British Embassy in Lirvob evacuated eighteen staff nationals which included Lloyd and his wife, Nona". As a result of their marriage, she had obtained a dual British Miyaland passport enabling her to travel to the UK. The evacuation was undertaken with an armed guard convoy, on route to the border. This being approximately fifty kilometres away from Lirvob."

Brian moved uncomfortably in his seat, "The report we have had is that on route the convoy came under fire from insurgents. During the attack, a rocket hit the vehicle travelling behind Lloyd's transport, and was completely destroyed. The explosion sent out shrapnel, hitting the vehicle in front, badly injuring Lloyd and one other occupant."

Gabriella gasped, putting her hand to her mouth.

But Brian carried on talking. "I'm afraid I can't be any more specific than that. The only other piece of information I can give you is that Nona, his wife, is on a flight into Heathrow, I think arriving tonight. I am sure we will know more by tomorrow."

Brian stood up, taking a couple of steps towards her, and putting his hand on her shoulder. "I'm really sorry it's not better news."

"Oh dear" said Gabriella "I do hope Lloyd will be all right"

"All we can do is hope and pray" said Brian 'I will let you know as soon as I hear anything."

"Thank you so much for coming. I appreciate it". Standing she led Brian to the main door.

"Will you be all right?" He asked.

"Yes, thank you, it's just the shock of it all".

Gabriella found it difficult to sleep that night, as the past occupied her mind. Accepting their divorce was one thing, but it still did not dull the pain. They had had a wonderful time together; she was now remembering all the good times. Then the involvement with this other woman, Nona; the tragedy of it all. She was not one for praying but that night she did. Waking early, she had a quick breakfast, showered, and dressed. Then, as usual, she put the Television News channel on, hoping there may be some update on Miyaland. The subject matter did not mention anything regarding the evacuation. She scanned the rolling text at the bottom of the screen. All it said was that more emergency talks were ongoing regarding the situation. All she could do is await some news from Brian. Turning off the television, she felt she must go outside.

Dressing accordingly, as the weather was overcast, she made her way to the park. On Thursday, hopefully things will send her life in a different direction, she thought, you cannot change the past.

That afternoon Angela came to see her. She was really intent on finding out what had happened after the Ritz encounter and had already phoned the previous day to find out, inquisitive about that man, the photography chap. What was the update? She wanted to be the first to hear.

Angela was surprised when Gabriella started off telling her the situation with Lloyd, and how he had got caught up in it. Angela listened intensely, wondering if it would take its toll on Gabriella. "Oh, You Poor Thing!"

Just then the phone rang.

"Hello, Brian Bradshaw here. May I come around as I have …" he paused, "… I'm afraid it's not good news.

"Please tell me Brian, I've been on tenterhooks all day. I have a friend here with me, so please tell me, is Lloyd all right?"

There was a sigh on the end of the phone, "I'm afraid Lloyd has died from his injuries, Gabriella, I'm so sorry."

There was a silence both ends of the line.

Angela sensing something was wrong got up out of her seat and came over, then put her arms around her friend. She could feel Gabriella shaking.

"Gabriella," Brian said, just as she was about to say goodbye.

"Yes, I'm still here"

"I don't know if this is the right time …" Brain paused again, "… the right time to mention that Nona has arrived in the UK, and has been taken to Mary Magdalene Hospital, Westminster. I apologise if I've said the wrong thing"

"Not at all. Thank you, Brian. I'll be all right. Goodbye."   With that, she put down the receiver and Angela guided her back to the sofa,

"I'll make some tea." said Angela.

The next day she arrived at the hospital, making enquiries at reception.

"Hello I've come to visit Nona" she paused, "Nona Richardson".

"Just a moment," said the receptionist "I'll make some enquiries."   After putting down the receiver, she turned to Gabriella. "May I ask who you are?"

Gabriella   hesitated.   "I'm   Gabriella Richardson," she replied, using her married name.

"I needed to know", said the receptionist, "as Mrs Richardson is in intensive care. I'll get a nurse to take you up."

Gabriella had taken a sharp intake of breath, "My goodness! Is she all right".

But by now the nurse was directing her towards the lift; while they ascended to the second floor, the nurse informed her about the patient's condition, and what to expect when she saw her. The nurse mentioned she was under sedation.   When the lift doors opened, they walked along the corridor to the Intensive Care unit.   "We needed to put Mrs

Richardson in IT, due to the trauma suffered following the Caesarean." The nurse said.

"Caesarean!" repeated Gabriella, stopping in her tracks.

"Oh sorry, I thought you would have known, as a family member. She was nearly full-term pregnancy, so it was decided best to deliver the baby, due to the severity of her injuries". Seeing Gabriella's expression, the nurse continued her explanation. Her baby girl weighed six pounds four ounces and doing fine."

Gabriella's expression softened. "The poor woman! What exactly is the situation?"

The nurse explained what she knew. "Mrs Richardson was flown into London following her evacuation from Miyaland and we were instructed by the Foreign Office to organise her stay here. We have to keep them informed of her condition. I'm afraid I don't know any more than that."

They had now reached the intensive care unit, the nurse reiterated. "I must tell you that Mrs Richardson sustained some bad injuries so please be prepared for her appearance".

"It will take some time for her recovery." the nurse continued. "I suppose the Foreign Office will arrange for the baby's care in the meantime."

The nurse's words did something to her feelings she had not experienced since her own children were born. She couldn't understand why. Gabriella was now standing in the ward looking at all the equipment surrounding the bed; it seemed horrendous - a multitude of tubes and wires. She felt her heart sink. This poor woman, this woman who had taken her husband but to whom she could bear no malice.

"She is under sedation," remarked the nurse, seeing Gabriella's reaction.

By now they were at the bedside, Gabriella put her hand out and touched the bed. It was as though she needed to make some sort of connection. Her feelings were bewildering; it was almost as if Lloyd was in their presence somehow connecting her to Nona. The nurse could see Gabriella's eyes welling up, so she stood back to give her a moment, moving over to the door to wait. After a while Gabriella composed herself, and joined the nurse. Outside in the corridor, the nurse then asked her, if she felt up to it, would she like to see the baby.

Gabriella took a deep breath. "Yes".

At the maternity unit the nurse handed Gabriella to the sister in charge, after explaining her visitor was Mrs Richardson a family member, and that she would like to see Nona Richardson's baby, then the nurse left the ward.

"You've come to see our little wonder girl?" asked the Irish sister. "She came out of the incubator this morning and is doing just fine on her own."

The sister guided Gabriella towards the row of cots lined up in the ward.

"Here she is, we've temporarily given her the name of Miya as her mother came from there."

Sister left her in front of the cot, as she fussed with one of the other infants. Gabriella looked down into the cot. There lying under a pink blanket was the little creature, wearing a pink knitted bonnet. A feeling flooded through her body, this little baby lying there so vulnerable. Her father was dead, her mother in intensive care, and in no position to care for her in the immediate future. What would happen to her? Putting her hand on top of the blanket she could feel the warmth of the small body. She had no rights to this baby, and yet she knew she wanted to be part of her life. She sensed a sense of belonging. This baby was Lloyd's flesh and blood. Gabriella felt tears starting to roll down her cheeks: her feelings - part sorrow and part joy - pulsing through her, she knew choices would have to be made.

"You have a wonderful granddaughter." The sister remarked from across the ward, jumping to conclusions.

Gabriella did not correct her, she just thought: yes, I have, haven't I?

A Bristol Souvenir

Takes pride of place in the west country
Where fame and fortune came to be
It's the town of Bristol City
So take that trip, come and see

Wander its streets and quayside
Guide books state history made of the tide
Some good some bad as of the time
It's all there before you, you decide

Brunel trail-blazed the railway West
SS Great Britain eventually came to rest
Planned the suspension of Avon Gorge
His achievements in time stood the test

Cabot crossed the oceans discovered Newfoundland
Aboard the Matthew sailed without cower
Past records show in slavery had a hand
In his memory a statue and a lookout tower

The Llandoger Trow Tavern by Harbour-side
Where R L Stevenson and Daniel Defoe took stay
Its atmosphere inspired them, penning stories
Treasure Island, Crusoe fame along the way

Wesley a man of faith preached, took a stand
In those days when Kings-wood was a darkened land
Holds family fame of school, hymn, and chapel built
Along with legacy, equality of rights still stand

Colston a man of trade who spent his wealth to show
On halls, schools, and roads now hold his name to tell
But he made his money from a living hell
His statue took a dip, from pedestal his status fell

Came to port barrelled casks, full of sherry sweet
Toast and raise a glass to cream quality of class
Rich in colour, a taste unique delightful treat
Bottled to be defined in Bristol Blue Glass

Arden Studios in recent time, with visual invention
Animation of characters reaching global attention
Holds pleasure to young and old with innocent fame
From small beginnings now awarded world acclaim

Banksy now known by name of international art,
Illusive like as the Scarlet Pimpernel plays his part
Came from illegal graffiti now still the same
Street Art made respectable now gives fame

A festival of different shapes and colours to ponder
Hot air balloons drifting in the big blue yonder
Not forgotten B A C place of Concorde came to rest
RR showed the world flight splendour of the best

Influence by worldwide ventures past and present
Its community diverse makes up this city residences
Many cultures shaping style and creative passion
Along with ship shape and Bristol fashion

Zoo, Museums, or Cathedral many sites to see
Now enjoy your time stop for a coffee or a beer
and, don't forget before you leave
Why not buy a BRISTOL SOUVENIR

Letter of Complaint

To: Environmental Department

Dear Sir or Madam.

I'm sending you this letter with a somewhat saddened heart and growing frustration. This is my third time writing to your department within the last six months. Appertaining to the problem we still have, as outlined in detail in my previous correspondence.

It has come to the point now that our patience is running out. It's a sorry state of affairs when situations like this have to drag on.

I hear your constant twittering on about underfunding, but surely you must realise, as my mother used to say "A stitch in time saves nine". Calculating the cost at this present time to put things right would be minuscule, compared with if left becoming prohibitive. We need action now.

The health of both my husband, and myself has somewhat deteriorated, due to the worry of it all. Consequently, we are now both under the Doctor receiving medication. I'm now on anti-depressants, the side effects of which have given me increased flatulence; this now has got to the point where it is affecting our more intimate moments. Not forgetting that my poor husband's blood pressure has risen along with the nervous rash, which has now come with its own additional problem concerning the cream prescribed. It is staining his underwear, and will not come out, even on a hot wash cycle. This is creating embarrassment, as I am unable to peg them outside, being conscious of the neighbours noticing.

Do we warrant this situation at our time of life? It has now gone beyond comprehension what do we pay our community tax for? Surely you must realise your responsibilities.

My husband and I would never condone or incite any form of violence in any shape or form whatsoever. But you know, as well as I do, that if this was a third world country, the placards would be out by now, and you would have a full-on demonstration on your hands, that would then more than likely turn into a riot. The consequences might be, that the likes of your department being pulled from your safe haven of offices, dragged kicking and screaming into the street, beaten and possibly thrown into jail. Or even held hostage for a ransom, until the problem was sorted. The worst scenario would be being put up against a wall and shot.

I know this is extreme, but you must realise the severity of what we are having to endure. I'm sure if *you* were living here, with your connections, it would have been dealt with post -haste.

The ultimatum is, that if we do not have some reaction to my letters within the next fourteen days. I will have no alternative but to approach our Right Honourable Member of Parliament for North East Somerset. Yes, I see you smile; because of his recently noted laid back attitude in the House of late. But I assure you, when he receives our notifications on your handling of our problem, it will certainly make him pull himself together and sit up.

Then you will get the full force of his supercilious tones, but eloquent tongue!

I state my case.

Your despondently
Mrs Haddy Knuff

A Wander in Sydney Gardens

An Oasis set in Georgian scape rest
A legacy in architecture displayed at best
Adorning structures set in green carpet lay
Meandering paths allowing you to stray

A park set of shrubs and trees
Botanist collected across seas
Species brought from far and wide
To survive the climate here reside

Majestic in design bridges span its water way
Father Thames meets Goddess Sabrina on display
East joins West, trade of yesteryear was done
Now railways pass in parallel service run

Take a wander see and feel a time to render
How articulately shown every vista's splendour
Enjoyment here for everyone with opened mind
Explore, you will be surprised what you will find

Come upon blossomed boughs, aroma fills the air
How delicate its form, nectar offered free to share
How brief a celebration of its beauty to view
Then gone is our time, so just say thank you

Hannah

The Cover Up

Hannah closed the hotel room door, hearing the dull click as it auto locked, then turned and walked along the corridor towards the lifts. She was on her way to a working breakfast with her agent, downstairs at the restaurant. *This was going to be the big one,* she thought. Arriving at the lift doors feeling a little flustered, she then decided to take the stairs; her room was situated on the third floor. This would give her time to calm and compose herself.

What a long way her career had come, with success now after all these years. The art world was very fickle; in her opinion it was controlled by a group of people in the upper echelons. Their word was god, they could make or dismiss an artist however great their talent. It was all a matter of opinion, about the trend that was set, and of course money.

Getting to the bottom of the stairs in the hotel foyer, she made her way across to the restaurant. Walking in she looked around, and saw her agent Neville sitting at a table located in a far corner. As she approached, he stood up to greet her.

'How are you?' he asked, as he bent forward to kiss her cheek.

Reluctantly she responded, despite detesting the smell of his overpowering aftershave. She assumed he must put it on by the handful.

'Fine, thank you.' she responded.

Neville was a man of medium height and rounded, a false smiley type. He spoke in a refined Midlands accent partly due to a university education, she thought, but no doubt over the years enhanced by mixing with the pretentious upper crust of the art world.

Seated, they ordered from the menu.

'Are you ready for the big day?' he asked.

'As ready as I'll ever be,' she answered after taking a breath, trying to stay calm.

'I know it was a rush, and you had to work late last night but I'm sure it will all be worth it. I just know it will be a success for you.' Neville encouraged. 'All those invites to the preview this afternoon, plus my contacts should shine through.' he added confidently.

Although she didn't care for his character, Neville had done well in building her reputation within the last two years. He had got her noticed in a number of high-profile exhibitions. Now, she was having her solo exhibition here in London's West End at the famous Bellom Galleries. With this step up in her career, she hoped eventually to reap some financial gain out of it all; this had eluded her so far, having to pay for presenting her work, fees to her agent and galleries, and high commissions on any sale.

While eating their breakfast, Neville went through some of the finer points regarding the exhibition. Her part being to present herself to the public. This was a role she would have to embrace whole heartedly, he stressed. Public relations were everything these days in the commercial side of the art establishment. This was something she hoped she would be able to handle.

Although she felt confident, an independent person and somewhat flamboyant in her dress, she was basically a shy person, and had no problem living on her own. Like most artists she had a hungry ego and a need to be recognised in what she enjoyed doing. Getting that feeling of release within her body, a self-fulfilment that needed to come out.

Her apprehensions came with the commercial side of the business. She felt a bit like a fish out of water, and feared that she may be easily drawn along a path where she would have little control

Her family had moved away from London after the war, moving to a new housing estate in the East Anglia garrison town of Colchester. She'd spent the later years of her education at the East Anglia College of Art and, after graduating she had worked for a local commercial design company, but still practiced fine art in her spare time. She had always wanted to be an artist in her own right.

As the years progressed, she worked in a variety of art and design type jobs, but was never satisfied working to other people's criteria.

Hannah had never married; relationships had come and gone. Really, she wanted to be a free agent, the restraints of a relationship had never worked in her life.

As she had aged her perseverance with her art had gradually paid off, the galleries had started to take her work. This had resulted in an almost sustainable income, along with her part-time teaching art at Colchester College, which she enjoyed and found rewarding through the enthusiasm of her students.

A few years ago she had moved, setting up home in a small village called Wivenhoe, east of Colchester, settling into a one-time fishermen's cottage situated on the eastward side on the bank of the River Colne. She had a modest-sized studio consisting of a lean-to built on the north side of the property. She loved living there with her Red Setter, Poppy, her number one companion.

Following breakfast, they both left the Hotel; Hannah's senses were immediately hit by the sheer noise and energy of the city streets. This was not her at all. With some resolve she would have to bear it. Luckily a taxi was waiting to whisk them away and once seated inside the noise subsided.

Arriving at the Bellom Gallery she walked in slowly, savouring the atmosphere. Here was her own exhibition in the heart of London. She passed through the layout of the gallery. This was her time just to relish seeing all her paintings on display. She felt a sense of achievement, it had been a year's hard work getting this together.

Her artworks were inspired by her surrounding countryside - its raw sense of nature with few trees set in the landscape. The East Anglian terrain being flat had little or no defence against the cold Eastern winds cutting across the North Sea from Scandinavian shores; there was nothing in its way to veer their path.

Most days she rose early to walk with Poppy. Her favourite mornings were in the Spring and Autumn. A time when the skies were still dark. Walking eastward she watched the yellow strip of light appear on the horizon as the sun began to rise. Then bit by bit the scene before her unveiled. It was magical watching the light catch the tips of long marsh grasses dancing in the prevailing breeze as the long sloping mud flats stretched along the river banks changed from dark brown sludge to the warm colours of the sky which were also mirrored in the river waters as they flowed gently seaward.

All this had become part of her, this love of nature with all its variations. The continuous change of the seasons, with all the wonderful shades of colour along with the wild life, which included the waterfowl flocking in variety and large numbers; all these comprised features for her to take in and then mix in the colours on her pallet to be transposed and expressed onto her canvases, creating those atmospheric scenes. This experience and ability gave her work her individual style, which had become recognisable in the world of art. This is where Neville had played his part.

The preview did not start until 2 pm so she still had a chance to make sure everything was to her liking, as the staff were still making things presentable.

By the reception area, Neville was talking to the gallery organisers. They had done well with the promotional side, including a beautiful brochure; some had already been sent to potential buyers. This had all been helped by Henry Althorp, an art dealer of some prestige. She had been introduced to him by Neville at the Exhibition in Brighton last year. He had bought a painting of hers for a client. Hannah felt this had been a step up in her career, as she was now being recommended by a dealer. He had mentioned to Neville at the time he had faith in her work, and the potential to go far.

As she wandered through the gallery she noticed a dark-haired lean gentleman wearing a dark blue suit. He was looking at one of her paintings. Seeing her approaching he abruptly walked away in the opposite direction. She wondered who it may be? The Gallery doors were not open yet for the preview. Her eyes followed his direction as he walked towards the exit. He turned and said something to Neville who nodded back.

Later with Neville she remarked on the puzzling incident. He just seemed to brush it off saying,

'Oh, he's an acquaintance of that dealer, um; you know Henry. I think he was in a bit of a hurry.'

Come 2 pm a small trickle of viewers started to come in; within the hour there was a throng of people.

'It all looks very promising,' said Neville, with a certain amount of relief in his voice.

They stood together in the centre of the gallery, a look of contentment on each of their faces, with the gathering showing a lot of interest, and also being plied with drinks.

Just then Henry the art dealer approached, immaculately groomed. She remembered him. Accompanying him was an elegant lady.

'Hello, may I introduce a friend of mine, Gabriella.' said Henry

Following their conversations, after a while Henry turned to Neville. 'May I just have a word, Neville?'

The two men wandered off to one side.

'These men and their business,' remarked Gabriella raising her eyebrows, following on saying. 'It must be so exciting for you to be here; I hope I'm not sounding patronising, but you must have a wonderful sense of achievement.'

'Thank you' said Hannah, she had taken a liking to Gabriella, and felt comfortable being left in her company. 'It's over a year's work, so I've got my fingers crossed. I'm not at my best in this environment; do you go to many Galleries?'

'Yes, I usually go along with Henry, I've known him a long time.' Answered Gabriella. 'I have one of *your* paintings hung in my apartment. It's of the sunrise and one of my favourites. I believe Henry purchased it at an Exhibition at Brighton. He said he highly recommended it. It's funny he has an uncanny way of knowing what people like.'

'Yes, he does seem very knowledgeable.' said Hannah

'It has been lovely to meet you, the artist in the flesh so to speak.' said Gabriella, touching her arm

'That's kind of you, it was nice to meet you too.' said Hannah, seeing Henry approaching, not that she wanted to end the conversation, but she had been instructed to mingle as much as possible.

'I hope we may meet again' said Gabriella, 'I will take a brochure and be in touch if you don't mind. Good luck.'

'That would be nice and thank you'. Hannah answered as she turned towards the throng of visitors.

For the next half an hour she mingled trying to do the PR bit as best as she could, though it all seemed so false. Then Neville met up with her, introducing a Mr Pollacov a Russian gentleman: a big tall man, round in face, and in stature. After their greetings, they spoke at some length about her work. He mentioned he was quite an eclectic collector of art, though old Russian art was one of his specialities.

'It has been a pleasure to meet you, Miss Roberts. Goodbye. No doubt our paths will cross again.' He ended by saying,

'Thank you, goodbye.' said Hannah with a smile.

Later Neville joined her again, this time to introduce her to the lean dark-haired man she had seen previously in the gallery.

'Hannah, I would like you to meet Signor Bruno Spezzia.' Neville said gesturing in his direction.

The man giving a slight bow of the head. 'Good day, Senora.'

'Hello' Hannah replied. She stopped herself saying, *didn't I see you earlier*.

'Bruno is from Venice and would like to discuss your exhibiting at the Viennalo, as part of the fringe Biennale Expo next year. He was looking to have three of your works but with some slightly larger canvases.' explained Neville

'Would that be possible?' inquired Mr Spezzia.

Hannah swallowed, *God* she thought, taking a deep breath. 'I'm sure I can accommodate you.' … trying to sound as calm as possible though her head was spinning with excitement.

'Well, if that is possible, I will arrange everything with Mr Neville and progress from there.' said Bruno confidently.

The rest of the day was a daze; she was walking on air. It ended with Neville buying dinner. As they sat at their table, she felt she could hug him, but perhaps that would be going a bit too far.

The preview, including the rest of the month, was a great success. Out of the forty painting she had sold twenty-five, the rest being taken by two galleries in London on sale or return. This was arranged by Neville. So, nothing to take home.

She was loving her time back in East Anglia knowing she could never be a city dweller. It was a relief to be away from the noise of the city. Mornings spent along by the riverside, with her faithful friend, Poppy, who she had missed so much. She was lucky to have Jack, her handy man, living down the road who was able to look after her Poppy if Hannah was away.

Back in her studio she was in her element. She had always wanted to paint larger canvases, but Neville had advised on saleable canvas sizes, due to his experience of the market. Doing these artworks, she felt, was a chance to really excel in her trade.

Over the next six months, she made ready the

paintings for the Venice show to the required dimensions advised. Neville kept in touch to ensure everything was going to plan, and kept her informed of the arrangements, shipping etc. Nearer the deadline, they had a discussion on pricing. This had always been one of her stumbling blocks, as to the price to put on her work.

Although as a recognized artist the value of her work had increased and she was now able to command prices in the thousands of pounds bracket, it was down to Neville to judge the market. He advised that she should put a price comparable to the venue.

He said, on reflection, as this was an international event, he would present the work at fifty thousand euros per painting.

'Are you sure, that seems a lot to ask.' Hannah said unbelievingly.

'Not at all, this is Venice the Biennale we are talking about, we must go for it. I know it's a gamble but there will never be another chance, this is all part of building your reputation.

Venice ... Biennale ... This was more than she could have ever imagined.

She had arrived in Venice yesterday not quite knowing what to expect. Neville had booked her into a grand hotel. Fascinated by the architecture of the city, she would have been happy to stay anywhere. It was Venice after all - what more could she ask for? Meeting Neville in the foyer after lunch, she walked with him out into the sunshine donning her shades as she went. As Hannah left the hotel, she suddenly became aware of the vibrant Mediterranean light which had enraptured so many artists through the ages, inspiring them to attempt to capture it in their work. Intoxicated, she drank in the atmosphere, feeling a touch of glamour she was not used to in the long flowing brightly coloured dress she was wearing, her hair tied up with a scarf as a turban.

Her next treat was the river bus along the Grand Canal towards the Exhibition, the reality of the setting delighting but also overpowering her. The Viennalo Exhibition was only two hundred metres away from the prestigious Biennale main venue, so Neville had noted, so the footfall should be good. The preview was going to be that evening; they were just going along to be nosey and check everything out.

Walking into the main hall of the Viennalo, again, she admired the architectural decor, it was a splendid venue. She could see the organisers and staff still busy titivating. As they wandered through, she felt daunted by some of the other artists' work, some of the names she recognized as having an international reputation within the art world. As they walked through the venue, she started wondering where her work was so Neville enquired where her paintings were displayed. It was the next hall along. Hannah breathed a sigh of relief. She knew from past experience that just because your work is selected there was no guarantee it would be hung, due to a number of factors. But there they were, all three of *her* paintings hung in all their glory. She had to pinch herself, were those paintings *really* hers?

The Grande preview gala was something special, even so she felt surprisingly at ease, determined to enjoy the event even if nothing became of it. Standing there beside Neville and Henry, she was introduced to various people of notoriety, and also noticed some famous faces in the gathering. She had a chance to speak to some of the other British artists, which she found fascinating, and was able to converse with ease. Then she was again introduced to the Russian Mr Pollacov; he said he liked her paintings, and was thinking about maybe purchasing one or maybe all three. She could not believe it, *this* man was going to spend one hundred and fifty thousand euros, on her paintings! He then told her they may be ideal for his apartments. Neville and Henry, must have worked their magic on him, she thought.

That night she couldn't sleep. It was unreal. She had come this far and now she could hopefully cash in on the international scene. This would set her up for life, along with the recognition she had only dreamt of.

The day came for the closing of the exhibition. She would go and see her paintings for the last time. Why not take a selfie with the paintings, as one does these days. Arriving at the venue, there were few people about. Walking straight to her paintings. She was shocked one of the paintings was not there.

'What's happened? Where has the painting gone?' She asked one of the attendants.

'Sorry, signora, I do not know.' he replied, looking as puzzled as her. 'I will go and ask.'

She now phoned Neville, expecting him to show great concern, but instead he said, 'I'm sure there's a perfectly good explanation.' and rang off.

On second thought perhaps he's right, she might be panicking about nothing. By now one of the officials was standing in front of her.

' Senora, the painting has gone to the workshop.' He said, speaking in a voice of authority.

'Whatever for?' she asked.

'I do not know it was just requested by the owner, Senora'.

'The owner … who is that?'

'Signor Pollacov.' speaking abruptly, the official turned about and walked smartly away.

So, he had purchased the painting after all! she thought.

It seemed all so mysterious. The good thing was he was the owner, so that was one consolation. She would phone Neville when she got back to the hotel as she needed to pack, her flight was early evening.

Later talking to Neville, he was pleased to say all three of the paintings had been bought by Mr Pollacov at the last minute. Henry had phoned him just half an hour ago to confirm it. He then confirmed that one of the paintings *had* gone to the workshop, but that's all he knew. After that Hannah was on cloud nine.

London - Two weeks later

Hannah and Neville ascended in the plush lift to the penthouse, the lift doors opening directly into the apartment. Stepping out they were amazed as they gazed out though the surrounding glass at the view - a panoramic cityscape, the light flooding across the floor. There to greet them was Mr

Pollacov and another man standing by him who she had not met before. Henry Althop was standing on the far side of the large room next to an easel supporting her artwork. The one she recollected that had been taken to the workshop in Venice!

'Lovely to see you, Miss Roberts,' said Pollacov, moving forward in greeting, shaking hands. 'Please come in,' gesturing towards the cream leather seating, offering them a seat. 'No doubt Neville has mentioned why we are all here.' he said, smiling in her direction.

'Only that, now you have acquired my paintings… sorry! your paintings, you wish to complete the deal.'

'Yes, of course. I think this calls for a drink don't you.' suggested Pollacov.

'No thank you I'm fine.' She replied, declining his offer.

Henry, moved towards them seated on the sofa, 'Hello again', he said, in his eloquent tones.

'Then let us proceed.' said Pollacov, giving a nod to the man not known to her.

The stranger then brought forward a briefcase, and laid it onto the low table set in front of her; he then retired.

'Please open it Miss Roberts,' Pollacov requested.

Hannah bent forward, placing her hand on the briefcase latches, thumbs pressed the knobs sideways. There was a simultaneous *click* as the top released, and she pushed open the lid.

An expression of disbelief sped across her face. Before her was a case full of neatly stacked bundles of bank notes.

'What's *all* this!', said Hannah, her voice

showing surprise.

'Well, we don't want to involve any taxman, do we?' Pollacov replied with a smile.

'This is not what I expected', Hannah remarked in a suspicious tone.

Pollacov turned. 'Henry, would you like to have a word with Miss Roberts

Henry stepped forward, 'My dear Miss Roberts. Hannah, I hope we are not faced with a problem.' A diligent look on his face, continuing, 'But surely you…'

'Sorry, but I don't understand.' Hannah interrupted. 'I'm not sure this type of business is for me'.

Hannah's mind was racing, all she could think of was: *this is money laundering.*

'You must face reality.' continued Henry. 'This has been a wonderful opportunity for you, don't you realise the time and effort that has gone into your debut in Venice. This is going to enhance your career; *you* should not take this lightly.' pausing. His persona had changed, his voice condescending. 'We have worked very hard on your behalf. A little gratitude would be welcome.'

'It's not that I'm ungrateful' she responded, 'I just want to know what this is all about.' Turning towards Neville she looked for an explanation.

Neville diverted his gaze away from her and said nothing.

Pollacov interjected.

'Don't worry, it's just we don't like to get involved with the Inland Revenue. that's all.' He said in a reassuring voice. 'They tend to ask questions.

'Neville here will work out all the banking details, I'm sure you will find them satisfactory.' Said

Henry.

Hannah felt flustered. 'Please, I'm having a job taking all this in'.

Another man entered the room carrying a bottle of champagne and glasses. He placed the tray on a tall narrow table next to the wall, proceeded to open the bottle, then poured out four glasses.

Again, Mr Pollacov tried to lighten the atmosphere.

'Please, come, we will have a drink to my new acquisition.' Gesturing them all towards the champagne.

All four of them now gathered around taking a glass, then all turned towards the painting set on the easel. The large canvas fixed to its boxed stretcher, unframed. Hannah now felt a touch of pride, as they all gazed upon *her* painting. She knew all the effort she had put into creating all three of the artworks. Perhaps she should take this chance, even knowing it was unethical. Now she had come this far, next time she may be able to call the shots. For her this was her moment of glory.

'May I ask.' Hannah enquired. 'Why was it that this particular painting was taken to a workshop?'

'Oh! we had it lined.' answered Pollacov.

That's funny, she thought, that procedure is usually applied in circumstances if a canvas is old or damaged, and there had been no mention of damage, or any sign which she could see. Without any further explanation to Hannah, Pollacov addressed them.

'Now you will see the fruits of their labour.' Turning to his man giving him the nod.

Hannah was still puzzled.

His man then walked towards the painting, whilst taking a scalpel-type knife from his pocket.

Facing the box canvas, he placed the tip of the blade under the edge of the canvas on the top left-hand side of the stretcher. Then proceeded to draw the blade down to the bottom corner, slicing effortlessly through the material. Then repeated this action on the right-hand side and then finally across the top. Hannah stood there transfixed as the top of the canvas, *her painting*, fell away, rolling down towards the floor like a giant scroll. A feeling of shear horror, then disbelief, as the canvas below was unveiled. She could hear Neville and Henry gasp, as they both took an intake of breath.

There before them was a masterpiece, a renaissance painting emanating a beauty even Hannah could not ignore, lost in amazement as they all gazed upon it, almost like an apparition of The Virgin and Child.

'This Lady and Gentlemen is *my* Bottalinne'. Pollacov announced with pride, breaking the silence.

As Henry moved closer for inspection. 'Ha! Ha ! You rogue!' he jested.

'Have no fear it was acquired by legal means.' Pollacov reassured them, 'It's just the Italian Authorities are a bit touchy when it comes to their native art works leaving the country.' explaining the situation.

Hannah knew she was looking at a painting worth millions in any western currency. No wonder paying out a mere hundred and fifty thousand was chicken feed to him. A feeling of claustrophobia came over her.

'Neville!' Hannah raised her voice, 'I need to leave, Now!'

'Please don't adopt that tone, Miss Roberts.' Pollacov said, turning to her. 'Your painting will not be discarded; it will be restored as good as new, to adorn my apartment.' He said trying to calm her.

'I do not want to be involved with any of this.' said Hannah, her voice raised.

Henry had turned around by now, the painting behind him, 'I'm sorry my dear but *you* are involved, as you put it.' His eyes in direct contact with hers. '*You* should be quite clear of your position in this matter.' His voice sounding fervently more menacing.

'Neville will explain how things work from now on.' announced Pollacov, in a matter-of-fact tone. 'That *is* the situation, goodbye, Miss Roberts'.

Hannah headed straight for the lift; she couldn't wait to get away. Neville followed in her footsteps, on the way stopping to close the top of the briefcase, then proceeded with it and its contents, quickly joining her.

As they descended in the lift Hannah was fuming. 'Did you know all about this? Did *you* help *set me up?'*

'I swear I didn't know anything about the other painting. I was as surprised as *you*. But surely if that's the way Pollacov wants to conduct business why should we worry. He still wants your painting; he'll have it reframed. What's the problem?'

'It's the principle of the thing, it just doesn't seem right.' her voice calm now.

'Hannah, this is business, what do you think this is all about?' he said, hoping to convince her. 'I know art should be appreciated, but the unfortunate thing *is* many artworks or masterpieces like that will more than likely never see the light of day, being locked away in some vault.' explained Neville.

'Why?' Asked Hannah, perplexed.

'Because to insure it for display would be astronomical for a individual collector. The next time it will most likely be viewed is at auction, sometime in the future. No doubt when Pollacov wishes to capitalise on his investment. It's like money in the bank to these people, but with a decent interest in today's climate. When it comes down to it, the whole art world would not survive without this type of thing going on, supply and demand.' Neville tried to justify what had taken place.

Sitting in the train homewards to Colchester, her thoughts and feelings were confused. How had she got engulfed in this! What could she do? It was all too much for her to comprehend. In retrospect she realised why she had been asked to submit paintings of a particular size, purely to accommodate his requirement. Reflecting now, how she had been used, she understood that it was no use looking for justice. This was real life in the art world.

What would be the best way forward?

In her heart, she wanted to leave it all behind and go back into her simple way of life. Is it worth all this stress? Along with the deceit, she thought, the joy had gone out of it. Like all artists she craved recognition for her art, but did she want the fame that went along with it? And having to be involved with those type of people? Perhaps if she were younger, she would be able to stand up and take it in her stride. It was a business just like any other ... but not quite. There were no built-in regulations. The people at the top in the know had a free hand. Millions in currency shifting around the world and nobody seemed to care. Should she just go with the flow, and enjoy her ill-gotten gain? Why not?

A new way of life living with extra luxuries, with no more worries about her bank balance. Just shut up and carry on. Unfortunately, it wasn't her, it was not right. She knew she could not live with the deceit. It wasn't just about morals; it was the damn complacency of those men having that kind of control over her. She had made up her mind; as soon as she got home, she was going to phone Neville and tell him all deals are off,

Back at Colchester Station, she retrieved her old car from the car park, and then drove home to Wivenhoe. Walking indoors she was glad to be home. What a relief!

A knock on the door and there was Jack with Poppy.

'Saw your car go by.'

'Oh, thank you, Jack, that's lovely.' as Poppy fussed about, she was all over her.

'She's missed you.' said Jack.

'I've missed her so much; she's my love. I don't know what I would do without her.' she said, hugging the dog.

'Anyway, I'll be off, wife's got the dinner ready, see you tomorrow morning then. Bye', said Jack, as he walked off down the garden path.

It was lovely to be home again with Poppy. I'll just have a cup of tea and then phone Neville. Her mind was back on track as to what she must do.

Phoning Neville she only got his answer phone, leaving a message for him to call her back.

After going for a short walk to breathe in the clean air - so much better than the stifling city with its noise - Hannah sat at her computer and Googled *Fraud Squad*. It came up with a local division situated at the Essex Constabulary, with email and contact phone number. Making a note, she decided to wait until she had spoken to Neville. Although he had said he hadn't known about what had gone on, she needed to know what position he would be in, giving him a chance to come clean. She knew he would argue his corner, and try to dissuade her, but she at least owed him that much.

It was nine o'clock that evening when Neville phoned her.

'Hi, got your message.' in his cheery voice. 'I've been sorting the finances out, so as near damn it your amount will be one hundred thousand. You will be able to filter it through a couple of accounts I've set up over the next twelve months, and of course you can always have some ready cash within reason. As long as we respect the situation, then we will be all right. I promise, and …'

'Neville! Neville! Stop it, *I cannot do this!'* cutting him short, her voice pleading

'What do you mean?' He retorted sharply.

She paused taking a breath. 'It's no good! I can't get involved with this'. Trying to be firm and decisive in her voice.

'I'm sorry but *you* are, we both are.' he replied. 'Don't you want the fruits of our labours? I can't understand you?' His voice softening.

Hannah just sighed with sheer frustration.

'Don't be stupid, I think you know what is for the best' said Neville his voice now firmer.

She was seething by now, she wasn't taking any more, she was going to stand firm. 'I'm warning you now, I am going to contact the Fraud Squad tomorrow.' She was now in a fighting mood, but starting to shake.

'Don't be a dammed fool, for God's sake sleep on it. You don't know what you are up against!' he shouted.

'I've made up my mind, that's it', she shouted back.

She hung up.

That night she had a difficulty sleeping as she lay in bed. She continued recounting the situation over, and over in her mind. At some time in the early hours, she must had dropped off to sleep. Next thing she was awake, the morning light coming through the window. She felt drained. With an effort she got out of bed and dressed. She could not wait to get out and walk the marshes.

Outside breathing in the morning air, she started off on her walk with Poppy by her side. This will clear her head she thought, so she could see reason in how she would state her case.

This was going to be her stand against what she felt was morally wrong. It may be common practice in the art world per se, but she had decided she did not want anything to do with it. I'm sure *someone* in the Fraud Squad will help me through this. She just felt stupid that at her age she had been deceived in this way. She should have seen the signs. All that going to Venice business - she should have realised it was too good to be true. Those men between them had manipulated her.

Poppy was enjoying the surroundings as she ran along the footpath ahead of her.

Hannah thought, *I should be here enjoying all this with Poppy, getting inspiration for my work, instead of my mind being full of turmoil*.

Back home she walked through her garden gate, closing it behind her; Poppy ran off around the garden checking her territories as she always did on returning from their walks. Hannah walked along the path which led to the cottage. Then she entered the stable door which opened into the kitchen. The morning air was warm by now, so decided to leave the top of the door open.

Oh! for a nice cup of coffee she thought, feeling a bit more relaxed, whilst hanging her top coat on the inside hook. She now busied herself with kettle and cup. Two minutes later she was pouring the boiling water into the cup, as she did so, she heard the sound of a vehicle in the lane outside. *Post early this morning,* she thought.

Walking to the door and poking her head out of the opened top section, she looked down along the side of the cottage. Her eyes travelled along the path towards the gate. Her heart stopped. Poppy was lying in a heap by the gate.

Rushing from the doorway down the path, panic set in as she arrived at the motionless dog. With pangs of fear running through her, she bent down to see what had happened to her lovely dog.

'Poppy! Poppy! What is it?' Gasping in alarm, tears now flooding her eyes, she raised the dog's limp head, its tongue protruding with excessive saliva coming out her mouth. In doing so she noticed, tucked under the collar a piece of folded paper. As she turned the dogs head it fell out and sprung open. Her eyes could just see through the mist of tears, the words in capitals: ASLEEP THIS TIME.

Her head was spinning, *it can't be, surely not!* The bastards!

As if on cue Jack was suddenly there, standing

on the opposite side of the gate. 'God! What's happened?'.

'I think she had a stroke or something.' She replied, as Hannah secreted the piece of paper into her shirt pocket.

'Is she breathing'? he asked

'Yes, can you help me get her indoors and I'll call the vet.'

Jack climbed over the gate, avoiding the prone dog. Then together they carried Poppy into the cottage placing her on the sofa.

'I'll call the vet.' said Jack.

'No! no it's all right I can do that. I think she'll be all right.

Just then the dog started to stir, her eyes starting to flutter.

'It's all right Jack, thanks, I'll just wait a while, then I'll phone and get the vet to check her over.' A feeling of relief came over Hannah, her voice steady now.

'Ok, give me a call if you need me.' said Jack, as he looked down at the dog moving and stretching herself.

After Jack had left, Hannah put her arms around Poppy realising full well what had happened. That was just a warning! How can these people wield that sort of menace? All for the sake of greed.

Sitting there with her it was over an hour before Poppy was fully awake. Poppy was her soul mate. She knew she could never sacrifice the only real love in her life.

Lockdown Garden

This space I go to sit in now
It's been there a long long time
I've never took much notice
only to use the washing line

It's my own back garden
It's really only a small plot
But what goes on out here
I thought time had forgot

Now we're in this Lock-down
Within this enclosure I reside
I know it's always been there
I'd never the time to realize

Sitting here I now observe
A place for other living beings
Of creatures great and small
Nature's business, it's worth seeing

A busy place to them, so vast
As creatures scurry to and fro
Carrying on their daily task
Amazingly they know where to go

Look! among the grass and bushes
A chance now this time to seize
Moments never taken to gaze before
Butterflies, flowers, leaves on the breeze

Always too busy, never time to sit
To watch birds, bees all come and go
No hurry now, slow down, just look!
Reflect on nature's life in natural flow

One Stop Romance

John boarded the train at Temple Meads Station. It was early afternoon. He had left work after a late lunch and was quite happy to finish the report at home as his company allowed him flexible working. Settling himself down next to the window, putting his laptop man-bag on the seat beside him, he observed, as expected at this time of day, that the carriage was only half full. Normally travelling to and from work he had to stand. This never bothered him as he only had to travel one stop along the track, to and from Keynsham to Bristol, on the Bath line. At twenty-two years of age, he had done well, working for a large insurance company in the city centre. Although he had had girlfriends, he was still unattached.

Glancing across to the seat facing him, he could not help noticing the young woman opposite. It was her soft smile that captured his attention and her eyes seemed as though they were actually looking at him. She *was* a beautiful young woman. He could see she was elegant by the way she dressed, with a silk scarf draped around her neck over a blue top which matched her eyes.

John became conscious of the middle-aged woman sitting in the other seat opposite, looking at the way he was staring. He turned and looked out of the window more than a little bit embarrassed and feeling his face flushing. After what felt like a decent while, he composed himself, then for something to do, fiddled with his computer bag, pretending to get some papers out.

God! those beautiful eyes - deep blue - and that soft, golden blonde shoulder length hair. He thought she must be a couple of years younger than him. As the minutes passed, he started to fantasise.

He knew he wouldn't in a hundred years have the courage to chat up a female of her style or looks; she was way out of his league. He was now becoming infatuated by her face. He momentarily held her gaze, dropping his eyes to look at those lips … with that smile.

John wondered what it would be like to have a young woman like her in his life. With a pang, he realised he would have to make his move. The train was now starting to slow its approach to the station. Would he ever see her lovely face again?

The train was now coming to a halt.

The middle-aged woman opposite was collecting her bags and things, including the fashion magazine that had been propped upright against her shopping, there, on the seat opposite him. That very magazine, with that beautiful female model pictured on its cover, which he had been gazing at throughout the journey.

John put his papers away, stood up, slipped his computer bag strap over his shoulder, then followed the middle-aged woman out of the railway carriage onto the platform. Once out of the station, John walked up the hill towards the town centre. There was a spring in his step, that magazine image still in his head.

Covid Reflection

Dark times as never known
This we have to bear
Rainbows in the windows
Remind us of those who care

Now gradually it's changing
We are opening our shell
Letting in the life we knew
 managed meetings, coping well

Many have lost what's dear to them
Without goodbyes, with so much regret
Now being one of the lucky ones
Having to move on, but never to forget

As the brakes come off bit by bit
 Moving forward, keep your distance
Especially consider the old folk
The ones with the less resistance

Is a new world waiting out there
To take on lessons learnt
Or will it all slide straight back again
Complacency, all resolutions burnt

Heed what may be around the corner
Ever prepared to face the unknown
Respect our position on this planet
Accept it, we are not alone

Getting to Know Henrietta Gardens

The month of May

Today's venture to green spaces starts under a grey sky; it looks like rain is on the way. With quickened pace along the uneven flagstones towards our destination, we all know where we are going, there's no hesitation and we soon arrive at the gardens-a central location in this city with easy access for all to come and go or use as shortcut passing through *en route* to somewhere else. It is set with pathways to follow, but also evident are the lines of desire of well-trodden grass where others strayed. Standing at the gateway I feel a sense of calm - enjoying this blessed chance to be out in the fresh air after all the months of our imposed detention due to the pandemic - along with heightened sense of interest to investigate our surroundings.

The terrain lies flat before us no effort to stroll here; This Oasis surrounded by its city dwellings, laid - out with scattering of various species of trees; some large mature; others small and willowy, accompanied with a variation of shrubs, adding to the light and dark uncountable shades amongst the greenery. All this vegetation giving shelter an abode where necessary to nature's creatures, their lives lived out within this space.

A change in the weather brings a brief period of sunshine, brightening the colours and deepening the shade, supplying a nuance, a more seasonal feel to our surroundings.

Wandering in an unplanned direction, letting the mind enjoy the journey without anticipation of the destination. Straying away from the laid-out pathways whose sole purpose is to reach a set end. I start to stroll on my chosen meandering route within this grassland, take time to observe the shrubs fully laden with leaves and flowers seasonal of the year. Giving attention to detail, taking note of the trees, as they block my path, notice how their trunks have formed, expanded over time pushing deep with their mighty roots and skywards with the force of their massive boughs. Observe also the textures of their bark from deep–cut scale-like features, to relatively smooth, almost soft looking inviting to the touch. Looking upwards to their structure of the branches; how they are so individual in each species and form. Their leafed canopies evolved through time for their life-absorbing needs.

Awed by the view of a monster horse chestnut laden with upturned blossom; its air of grandeur liken to a giant chandelier; beneath which coolness prevails, the dense foliage blocking out the light from the sky.

Many of these large trees that reside here have seen decades come and go, surpassing generation including my own span of life, as they live and grow; continue to give a presence to this place. A space designed and created, as many others by man for people of all ages to enjoy and observe nature flourishing in these built-up areas, allowing all manner of creature to live and breathe here.

Set within this parkland the memorial gardens in commemoration of King George V. Regimentally laid-out with flagstones underfoot surrounding a rectangular pond, set with accommodating seating running either side at various spacing, divided by a combination of trellis climbers, together with flourishing flowerbeds. This dedication in formal style is not to my liking, seeing nature so constrained to man's desire.

Now resting, seated on a bench, I begin to realise how much these green open spaces have become part of our culture, almost to be taken for granted; without them we would feel an unprecedented loss to our mental, and physical well-being.

Here, this public place provides a sense of tranquillity. Giving solace from the pace of life outside these garden boundaries, a place where people are able to enjoy this offering of peaceful pleasures, to release or relieve the frustrations and the stresses. es. An invitation to recreation to indulge in walks with the dogs, to meet with friends, or just to sit peaceably. No qualification required to these ends.

Our skies have now become overcast again, and rain is falling steadily.

Although I am not a lover of getting wet, it does not dampen my spirit of enlightenment, and I am left with my thoughts of the day. Thank you, Henrietta Gardens.

Molly

Double Love

Lying back in her armchair, Molly was awake now, although her eyes were still closed, still savouring the remnants of her dream. It had been nonsensical as most are, but Tom had been in it, with her. It had brought back so many fond memories, from all those years past. A loving tender man, he had given her so much, to a part of her life.

"Mooleee, my dear! here I have your morning coffee." the Eastern European accented voice penetrated the moment; it was Olga. "It's big day for you today, yes?" Placing the tray on the small table beside her.

Molly smiled as she opened her eyes, "Yes," half sighing, wondering to herself, how she had managed to live this long, her birthday, ninety years today.

"Look, all your lovely cards and party later," Olga reminded her. "And all your family coming also, yes?"

Molly smiled and nodded, bending forward to sip her coffee.

"We must sort you a dress and makeup later: after lunch I come." said Olga, as she was leaving the room.

Sitting there enjoying her morning coffee, Molly looked around the room situated in the nursing home. This had now been her home for the best part of the last five years. The room was a reasonable size, allowing her to have a small collection of her own belongings and knickknacks dotted about. She would have preferred to have stayed at her own home, but had been swayed by the family; it was for the best. She had managed to settle in well, and the staff were so nice to her.

Finishing her coffee, Molly relaxed, settling her now fragile frame back into the armchair. Her hands together on her lap, rotating her wedding ring with her right-hand thumb and forefinger. She remembered the day it was put on all those years ago. Married at eighteen to a man who had made her laugh so much, a Jack the Lad, as they say, although his name was Danny. He was twenty-one, working in the docks just as his father had done. Marriage then was as things just happened, at a time of life when the brain has little or no control. The naivety of those days, when that's what girls did, just got married to a good catholic boy, as a way of life.

In those days, no one told you or knew how it was all going to pan out. A career was unheard of for a woman, set in this restricted catholic community. This was Liverpool in nineteen forty-seven, in an overcrowded slum area close to the docks. The second world war had not long been over. A lifestyle set in rows and rows of terraces, everyone trying to make ends meet. A set culture of a man and his woman.

It had been all love and passion when they had first married, but as with most relationships, as time passed you either grow together or grow apart. It wasn't as though their marriage had problems, it just started to become a routine relationship, as many do, not really expecting anything else. Neither person thinking or caring to make it any more than what it had become. The lovemaking was now mostly initiated by him, on returning from the club after closing hours on a Friday night. A routine only, with a growing lack of tenderness or foreplay, which had now become nearly non-existent. Her own tiredness did not help any, and the money worries were always there - with no birth control in sight, along with catholic indoctrination. By the time Molly had been married three years she already had two babies and another on the way. Her life wasn't much different from most she knew, most woman in the area just had one child after another.

But this had only been part of her adult love life.

It might not have been perfect, but if the

money situation had been better, it would have been manageable. When the docks were working with plenty of shipping they got by. But times came with the strikes, with the pickets, and Danny being laid off. It was these disruptive situations that consequently found the shipping being diverted from Liverpool to other ports. By the time things got back to normal again, the problem then was trying to repay the debts which had accumulated.

Her Danny had been a good man. He was always laughing, always the optimist. Things could only get better and he never seem to worry. Always had his drink when he could and also a bit of a flutter on the horses - that's what men do when they get together. But, at times, it meant there wasn't much left in the kitty. They never argued, they just had to make do, though sometimes Molly would pretend she had already eaten, just so there was more food to go around.

In those days most families in the community had used the Tally man. It was the only way of holding things together financially. The children's clothes along with all the other essentials. Every week he would come around, lend and collect on what you had borrowed, a pittance in today's money, but so much then, and so many depended on it.

That's when Tom came along, a nice man, in his forties. Well dressed, able to live in a better part of the city. He had been calling in the area for the last eighteen months. After a while getting to know her, he used to stop for a cup of tea on his rounds when time allowed. As time went on, they used to chat about all sorts of thing. It was then he had spoken about his wife being in a sanatorium, suffering from tuberculosis which she had contracted some ten years ago. They never had any children, so in some way made it easier to cope, for him to do this type of work. Always having the weekends free to spend time visiting her. Molly had felt sorry for him having to fend for himself; he said he managed, but was grateful for her concern. She just wished she could have afforded to cook him something to take home.

Molly's memories slowed, revisiting that very moment when things had altered.

The money had become short again. Everything had all seemed to go downhill. Desperation had set in; the debts had built up and there was no money left. She still remembered that day vividly; the day everything changed.

"Look Molly I can't extend your credit, it's six weeks in arrears. That's more than I should have allowed you anyway. My boss is going to go crackers at me."

Tom was trying to be firm but his face did not reflect it. He found it hard as he always had been kind in his manner towards her. She now recalled how they had stood in the hallway facing each other, he with his top coat and trilby on, ready to leave. He stood there just looking into her eyes. She was now conscious of the tears that were running down her cheeks, knowing full well she had no way of paying, no way out of this mess.

She then had done something that was completely against her character and moral upbringing. Taking his hand in hers she pulled it towards her, resting it on her breast. Tom withdrew his hand immediately. She had felt a complete shame come over her; she was lost. But then Tom had thrown off his trilby and put his arm around her. With his other hand he gently tilted her head as his mouth was on hers, kissing her tenderly. She could not control her body; it had not felt like this for ages, all he wanted was to kiss her and hold her in his arms.

Bewildered. *This was not what this was all about.* She thought.

"Oh Molly!" she heard him say, 'please forgive me, you are such a kind and lovely woman."

Molly said nothing. All she did was stroke the back of his soft fair hair while holding him close. It just felt wonderful.

"Molly I've always had a soft spot for you, but I've got no right to take advantage." His voice being so soft towards her. "I'm sorry … it's with Jean being in the sanatorium so long. I've been so alone. You must forgive me."

"Tom, it was me, please don't think badly." She had said.

Gradually they both composed themselves.

"Look, don't worry. I'll sort something." Tom said, reassuring her.

Things changed after that moment; everything seemed to get better. Danny was now doing well workwise, which helped the money situation. Gradually the debts managed to be sorted out. As the following months passed it was quite strange. The new baby arrived and Tom was so caring of how it was for her, each time he came he would always bring something for the children. Following his visits, they would always have a kiss and little cuddle, before he went. Molly became really fond of him and looking forward to them seeing each other. They were just like very dear friends then.

Molly knew this was a sin to feel this way but after she'd been to confession and performed her penance, she felt all right with her conscience. The Father seemed to always ask for more details when she confessed, questioning her over and over to make sure she had repented everything.

One day Tom asked her if she would come to his house to keep the place up together, as his house-keeper was retiring. He stressed that even if she could only come a couple of days a week, that's if she could get over on the bus, he would drop her back in the evening by car. And he would be able to pay her as a job, which would help her out financially.

She had checked this was ok with Danny, and being as how her two older boys had now started school, it meant she could take the baby boy Billy with her. It was easy to get to his home, only a fifteen minute bus ride. This was a chance to help Tom for all his kindness he had given her.

His house was a small semi set in a nice area away from the docks. Modestly furnished, it was easy to clean. She loved touching his things when tidying around. One thing she had been able to do was cook him nice meals, at least on those two days; he was so grateful.

So, over the next two years she had gone regularly to Tom's house - always on a Wednesday and Friday – and Tom would drop her back home. She had been so pleased with having a job, with some money of her own.

Then she remembered THAT week.

It had been the Monday, a couple of weeks before Christmas. Tom hadn't called in as usual on his rounds; nobody had seen him about in the neighbourhood. The following Wednesday she caught the bus, only this time she left little Billy with her aunt worried that there may be a problem.

Molly had arrived at the house and let herself in, knowing the hiding place for the key. Tom was not there; she then busied herself around the house going through some of her routine chores.

She felt a sudden warmth as she remembered the next scene so vividly.

It was about midday. She had looked through the window and had seen Tom walking up the garden path, his body language alone indicated something was not right. As he came through the door, she hurried to meet him. His face was sombre, his eyes red,

"Tom, what is it?"

"It's Mary … she had a relapse and died." he said mournfully.

"Oh, Tom, I'm so sorry." By now, she was helping him off with his hat and coat, then walking with him through to the sitting room. "Sit down, I'll make some tea." she said as she walked off to the kitchen.

Returning a little later with the tray, she sat down opposite him.

His body was hunched over, his head in his hands. She could see he was trying to hold back the tears.

"There was nothing I could do. I feel so hopeless." His voice was full of remorse. "Mary had suffered so long … if only I …"

"Tom, please don't go blaming yourself." Molly interrupted.

"I know," he said, "At least she is at peace now." With that his tears just flowed uncontrollably with the devastation of grief.

Awkwardly, she had risen from her seat and stepped towards him. Without hesitation, Molly bent down placing her arm around his shoulder. She so much wanted to comfort him. His head against her chest, bending her head downwards she kissed the top of his head, deep into his fair hair. On impulse, not knowing what to say to console him, she knelt down before him and started to kiss his face tasting the salt on his skin. Then, eager to ease his pain, she pulled him tight towards her.

Eventually, she rose, pulling him to his feet. Filled with such mixed emotion, she took his hand, and had led him up the stairs to the bedroom. There was no resistance in him; he had been in a daze. They stood by the bed and she kissed him deep on the mouth. As they kissed, they gradually removed each other's clothes. Not a word was spoken. Pulling back the covers, they had slid into the bed.

They were both naked; driven by a longing of something that could have happened long before this moment. No thought of whether it should be happening now. There was no rush in their love making, it had felt right just to hold each other with soft caresses. Eventually, it all seemed so natural as their bodies became one. This timeless void was theirs, as sleep overtook them.

Molly's eyes had opened first. Tom was still asleep beside her. Looking at the clock she saw that it was now late-afternoon. She would have to go. There was nothing more to be said.

After going to the bathroom, she dressed and tidied up Tom's clothes. Walking round to Tom, she bent and kissed him on the forehead. Then, taking the small gold cross and chain from around her neck, she placed it on the pillow where she had laid her head.

On the bus home, she had realised how much she loved Tom, but had recognised that her love could never be fulfilled. She loved her children; her family was her life. She would go to confession and repent. But would never forget.

The following Friday she didn't take the bus to Tom's. She would be strong.

The following Monday, a letter arrived from Tom. He said he had been so overcome by her kindness and would always remember her. He had decided to sell the house and move to London to live with his older sister, as she had been widowed during the war and was living on her own.

Molly had realised it was for the best; although her life would never feel the same. In the next few weeks, she knew she was pregnant again. Within the year, Molly gave birth to a baby girl. They had named her Tammy. Danny was over the moon, completely besotted by her. He said he would have to find a bigger place for the family to live, wanting something better where they could bring up their little girl. And besides, there were six in the family now.

As if by a miracle, two days later Danny came

back from the pub with the news that they were looking for new employees at the Port Sunlight Factory, Lever Bros. He had arranged to go for an interview the following Friday.

Everything changed after Danny got the job. Going over on that Mersey Ferry was like going to a different world. Danny and Molly were going to live at Port Sunlight, a place specifically built for the factory employees. Beautifully laid out in country village style with trees and greens, it had a community hall and its own railway station. It had been wonderful belonging to the community it had become.

Her memory paused as Molly remembered one special, personal moment from that time. She had been walking around their new home for the first time, opening one inside door, and there – she had seen the bathroom. That was one luxury she would never forget. Running the hot tap for the first time and then lying down into that bath full of hot water. Heaven!

As time had gone on their whole way of life changed. They all ended up working at the soap factory. A so much healthier lifestyle than she could have imagined for the family. Over the years as the children grew up and started their own married lives, she had become a grandmother to five grandchildren.

It was in the January of 1988 she had received a letter from a London firm of solicitors acting on Tom's behalf. It informed her that he had died that Christmas. They now required some identification regarding his will, as she was a beneficiary. Some weeks later after sending the required paperwork she had received a registered envelope. It contained a cheque for ten thousand pounds. When Danny saw it, he found it a bit puzzling. He remembered Tom coming to their home and also Molly doing housework for him all that time ago.

"Tom never had any children and I suppose his elder sister must have passed on; anyway, there could have been other beneficiaries of the will we don't know." Molly had argued convincingly.

Danny had shaken his head. "I know he was a good friend, but I still can't see how come you'd be in his will." he had said, still pondering. "Isn't that funny you getting that money after all this time."

But Molly knew in her fondest thoughts that Tom hadn't forgotten her after all this time, just as she had *never* forgotten him.

Later that year they had used the money to buy a bungalow in the suburbs and on Danny's retirement they moved to it. That was some twenty-two years ago now. Danny had passed away in 1998. All this time they had gone on and survived all the ups and downs of their married life. They had enjoyed a lovely life together, surrounded by all their family,

Coming back into the present, Molly looked at the clock on her sideboard. She had had her lunch and was now relaxing in her room.

Knock! Knock!

Olga popped her head around the door. "Moolee I've come to get you ready for party, now, yes?"

Over the next half an hour Olga fussed around Molly, both enjoying the challenge doing her make over.

"There now you look, as say ready for Queen, yes?"

Molly looked in the full-length mirror on the wardrobe door and smiled with delight, "Thank you, Olga my dear, I'm as ready as I'll ever be."

"Do you like me to take you in the wheelchair, or you like to walk?" Olga enquired.

"We will walk down together." replied Molly, "you are so good to me. You must come to the party. I want my family to meet you."

As they made their way along to the dining room, Molly marvelled: *all this is for me and all I've done is live my life. Everyone has skeletons in the closet, which is all part of the tapestries of life. Mine was just extra special.*

The double doors of the dining room swung open to a tremendous cheer: there they all were to greet her. Balloons, streamers everywhere - the staff had done her proud. They had given her a chair in pride of place, all decked out with ribbons and flowers. Here she was: Mother, Grandmother, and Great Grandmother.

Everyone gathered around her, giving her their presents, a great joy amongst them all as she opened them. A lot of nice things, some handmade by the grandchildren which she especially appreciated. Then came the cake - again the staff had excelled - with a loud chorus of *Happy Birthday* filling the air with song.

Now, one by one each of her children came forward to show their love and appreciation with a hug and a kiss. First her eldest, Michael, then Shaun followed by Billy, then the last of her brood, Tammy. Although you shouldn't have favourites, Molly couldn't help but think her daughter had grown to be a loving, caring girl. Although married, she always had time for her Mum and was always ready to help others.

As she bent forward to kiss her mother, pushing her long fair hair back over her shoulders, Molly saw the light catch on the small gold cross hanging from the chain around her daughter's neck. It had been a present Tammy had received on her twenty-first birthday. A package bearing a London postmark. At the time, she had been puzzled, telling her mother that, although there was a card with the present offering congratulations with fondest love always, there hadn't been any name of the sender. Even though Tammy never found out who sent it, she always said that she felt a feeling of love and protection wearing it. Molly had never mentioned to Tammy its origins. Somehow, Tom must have been able to find out and followed our progress in life. He'd never interfered, just wanting to pass that affection on. Tammy had certainly inherited his eyes, but Molly had never said anything to her.

All the rest of the children came forward in turn and gave her a kiss and a hug, enjoying each other's company, along with the refreshments. By late afternoon, everyone had said their goodbyes and Molly was on her way back to her room; tired now, Olga pushing her along in the wheelchair.

"Wasn't that just lovely for you? All those beautiful children, you very lucky lady." Olga remarked.

Back in the room Olga helped Molly undress and wash, changing into her nightdress and dressing gown.

"Thank you so much, Olga. I will have a lie down on the bed now, I feel very tired." said Molly listlessly.

"Ok my dear, I'll see you tomorrow. The next shift will be on soon and they bring you a cocoa soon ok, Bye." said Olga, as she closed the door.

Molly laid on top of her bed, her eyes closing almost immediately. Her life memories passed before her. She was at peace with herself now, and her family. As the sun set on her ninetieth birthday, it was all done, there was no need for tomorrow, and, for Molly, there was no tomorrow.

Town On a Hill

Unique this place set between two cityscapes
Settled on hilltop plateau, holds its place
Somewhere here the Roman's marked their spot
The Abbey that once played its part
Along with chocolate factory not forgot

Time has passed with its history of brass
Mills with water wheels still turn, hold fast
No sweat on brow, for thirst of hard work done
Places of leisure, hospitality they've become
To feast and drink in afternoon or evening sun

I first heard your name on the airwaves 208
Spelt out by Horace, football pools to per-mutate
Later rode the Bailey bridge in the years after '68
Many times, always passing through, no bypass then
Dashing East to West working, no stopping, late

How was I to know back then I would come and stop
In later years would settle in the town upon a hilltop
St John's bells call the faithful: christenings, weddings and
parting days.
Its towering structure marks this town's highest spot
Where constant movement at this junction plays

This town is my size, it suits me fine
Convenience at its best, could even say sublime
Walk the High Street for a coffee or a cake
Also pubs, clubs and restaurants, choice served
It's all there, if you want to stay out late

Take a walk down in the park the river running through
Rushing water, spot the wild life, as ducks paddling too
Wander among the trees, catch the breeze feel akin

Sit stop awhile, in the place where I've come to live
This town now part of me **K- E- Y- N- S-H- A- M**

The Legend of the White Horse

Chorus
There is a legend; There is a legend
Of a white horse which roamed these plains
And that spirit of the white horse
In the county still remains

Long ago in times gone by
A spirit flowed through this land
Tales are told of a mighty white horse
That gave the folk a common band
Its presence touched their hearts within
Revered in wonder its strength with pride
And through the years across this land
Carved its image in the green hillside
Chorus

Reflecting through the bygone age
The legend and the times they follow
Each has taken up the power
Hoping for that new tomorrow
Look now upon these rolling hills
The white horses, they're with timeless grace
That can be seen from far and wide
Has now become their resting- place
Chorus

In the morning mist you may glimpse
A ghostly form with flowing mane
Or its silhouette against the sunset
Its free spirit too wild to tame
Sometimes you may sense a feeling
Within these hills surrounding view
That you belong here in this land
And that spirit is part of you
Chorus

Now is the time to recall that tale
In this most beautiful of our land
To guard that memory for the future
Together hold each other's hand
Then let's once more light that fire
That drives the soul inside with force
And bring that feeling all around us
The spirit of the white horse
Chorus

Summertime

Everything is lighter brighter
that lifts the heart and calms the soul
Summer's here;
shrug off those winter months that took their toll
Turn off that artificial need of heat,
unwrap those weary hands and feet
Without these long lazy sunshine days,
our year is not complete
Now is time for the body to receive
to breathe, embrace, expose
Take chance, be brave, dispense
with bulky winter clothes
Past days endured of SAD syndrome
of now forgotten winter blues
Get out the shorts and flimsy frocks,
wear sandals instead of shoes
Give treat to all those hidden parts
that long to see the sun
Awareness of that healing process
that has now begun
Let limbs absorb Nature's warmth,
with hope of healthy gains
With every possibility
to ease those aches and pains
Maybe time for holiday
heal tired limbs or mental stress
Climb hilltops high to stand and view
let gentle breeze caress
Walk through woods with dappled glades
to valleys far below
Follow winding footpaths

where streams to rivers flow
Take time, hear nature's song,
instead of man-made noise,
To trickling waters or flapping wings
of dabbling ducks or swans poise
Stroll beaches, paddle
as temperate seawater subsides
Hear the shingle as it rolls
to and fro on ebbing tides
Coastal pathways up on cliffs,
calling gulls and gannets cry
Watch nature's display: circling buzzards
gliding high in cloudless sky
Rushing waves with timeless joy
crash upon the sand
It is all here for senses to taste
in our green and pleasant land
So, grab the chance, have your fill,
all free for the taking
Summer fair with its feast abundant
satisfaction in the making
Filled with fun, joy, laughter,
Enthusiasm, no time to restrain
Even if the weather forecast says
tomorrow it might rain

The Fund Raiser

Phone rings.

"Oh, hello Margaret. So lovely to hear from you."

....

"Yes, we did, last Sunday."

...

"Yes, I know, the weather was gorgeous, it couldn't have been better."

...

"What? Oh, yes, looking back *I* thought the fund-raising garden party was a marvelous idea and also a great success ... apart from that unfortunate incident with Dennis. Personally, I don't think Mary should have brought him considering the state of his health."

...

"Hmmm, it wasn't just the fact of him having a heart attack, but it was that it happened right in the middle of Mabel's appeal speech for the Heart Foundation Charity."

...

"I know ... and also to make things even worse he fell right into the buffet. Created such a mess."

...

"Oh yes, thank goodness everyone was so congenial, helping the catering staff clear up and put things right."

...

"Yes, wasn't it."

...

"Fortunately, there was limited damage, eats wise. It was the sandwiches, and finger rolls which were mostly deemed inedible."

…

"Yes, it was a shame."

…

"However, the wonderful array of cakes and deserts survived. Everyone seemed to love those and enjoyed themselves all round,"

…

"Oh yes, *they* all were so generous. By the end of it all, we managed to raise the grand sum of one thousand eight hundred and fifty-one pounds, and fifty-one pence."

…

"I know, wasn't it fantastic. Anyway, must dash Margaret, you know busy, busy!"

…

"What? Oh! Dennis? Unfortunately, he died later at hospital."

…

"The funeral? Next Thursday at Lastgate Crematorium, eleven o'clock, no flowers just donations. See you there! Byeeee!"

Left with a Dream

I saw your beauty when we first met
The signs I misread I thought you keen
Now my loving feeling turned to regret
Then I realised you were not part of my scene

All I'm left with is a dream
All I'm left with is a dream
All I'm left with is a dream
Of a love that could never be

You said you liked my company
I wanted to hold you tight
You hope we would be friends
I wanted you to spend the night

All I'm left with is a dream
All I'm left with is a dream
All I'm left with is a dream
Of a love that could never be

Seeing you with your kind of love
We laugh and joke I just put on a face
But inside I still have the longing
Could I find a love that will replace

All I'm left with is a dream
All I'm left with is a dream
All I'm left with is a dream
Of a love that could never be

Maureen

The Cellar

Set in the late 1960s ...

Maureen walked out of the fish and chip shop it had started to rain: a late November Friday evening, getting dark already. The bus had been late coming from town, so getting fish and chips would save cooking tea.

She pulled up her collar as she set off walking quickly, soon turning the corner on to her street. She glanced across at the pub situated on the other side of the street corner, it was still closed and boarded up; like many of the houses in the area, it was due for demolition. After all these years soon to be redeveloped.

She walked along the pavement stretching out before her with rows of terrace houses on either side of the roadway. The street lamps had come on, the wet pavement reflecting their light. There were no people about, and only a few windows were illuminated due to the small number of residents in the street now. All the families had been moved out already, re-housed on the new Princes estate. In the next fortnight, she would also be moving into her new flat there, having taken the next week off work to pack up her things ready to move. She had been looking forward so eagerly for all this to happen, to leave the old house.

She put her head down against the rain, quickening her pace again, thinking: *she should have taken the brolly.* The forecast had said wet and windy later that day. Two minutes later and she was home, opening the front door, switching on the light. Closing the door behind her, she took off her coat and said hello to the cat running into the hall to meet her. She bent to stroke its back then walked through into the sitting room, drew the curtains and turned on the gas fire. The evenings were getting colder, she'd need it.

Stepping through to the kitchen, she put the kettle on. While unwrapping the fish and chips, she felt the cat rubbing against her legs, which gave a lovely feeling of comfort. The cat knows it will be sharing her meal.

After eating, she cleared away and went into the sitting room closing the door behind her. By now the room was snug and warm with the heat from the gas fire. After switching on the television, she dropped into the armchair, the cat jumping up and immediately occupying her lap.

Feeling the heat coming from the gas fire onto her legs, she smiled, pleased that she had had the fire installed ten years ago. Before then it meant lugging the coal from the cellar to keep the open fire going.

She knew that, even after all these years, there was coal from the last delivery still piled in the cellar. But the door had been locked and not opened in all that time. The heaped-up coal covered a secret she had lived with, almost in denial, as the years passed.

Everything was better now. Her recovery from the living hell of a life she had led had been slow, taking several years. But within the next fortnight she would be moved into her new flat on the Princes Estate and able to take the cat with her. She just couldn't wait to move, *better now, better **now*** she thought.

All of a sudden there was a loud bang from the outside of the house. Something must have blown against the front door, but the sound had aroused dark memories from the past. A shiver went through her bones as it all came flooding back, remembering Friday nights after the pubs closed, then waiting for the footsteps outside the front window and the front door crashing open, then the sound of his shuffling body coming along the hallway.

What would lie in store for her this time? Would she be able to pacify him before he picked fault with whatever obscure thing had taken his fancy?

She had always tried to keep the house together, careful to make sure everything was to his liking. The trouble had all started two years after their marriage. His mother had died and he began to change.   His drinking became more excessive, especially on Friday evenings after work.

It had started from little niggles which became arguments, then verbal abuse.   Eventually, it progressed to physical abuse and those awful, outright beatings.   Blows were usually aimed at her body, bruises she could conceal from prying eyes, or the pulling of her hair.   Occasionally, blows would catch her face and she would stay indoors, or use makeup to cover the abrasions.   She always made excuses to inquiring eyes, knowing full well they were not believed.   Time had healed her and helped dulled the memory, but she still remembered living in fear.

That fateful night 10 years ago … she had fallen asleep in front of the coal fire and when she had awoken was horrified to find the fire had gone out.   Panicking, as he would not be pleased if he returned and found there was no fire alight in the hearth, which would give him yet another excuse to turn on her.   Her body had been shaking as she grabbed the coal scuttle and hurried to the cellar door; switching on the light, she descended the rickety wooden steps.

There was plenty of coal, a new delivery had been made just the other day.   A large amount for the cold winter months had been dropped through the manhole cover set in the pavement which funnelled down onto the cellar floor.

But then she had frozen, the fear rising inside her as she heard the front door bang shut.   He was in the house.   She had heard him shuffling on the floor above as he stumbled into the kitchen then lurched into the sitting room.   Instinctively she knew he would see the dead ashes in the hearth.

'Where are you?' he had shouted, 'Where are

you? Where are you? You ****!'

There had been silence down in the cellar; the only sound her heart racing. While above she had heard the sound of his heavy breathing almost like the snort of a bull ready to charge. He must have seen that the cellar door was open and the light on inside. She could almost hear his thoughts: *Someone will have to be taught a lesson.*

As he had lurched forward at the cellar doorway, one foot had slipped on the top step and he had missed his footing to the second step. As he had tried to steady himself with his right hand against the wall, he had caught the light switch and knocked the light off. Then, as if in slow motion, his whole body had become airborne just for a second, followed by the sound of his entire bulk crashing down on the bottom step; then the dull thud as his head had hit the concrete floor.

She'd held her breath in the deadly silence that followed, cowering in the dark against the wall. Gradually, as her eyes became accustomed to the light that seeped down from the kitchen doorway, she had seen his crumpled body lying there, motionless, silent.

Creeping from the corner towards him, a mixture of panic and relief came over her. His body had still not made any movement. The heavy silence had been broken as a sudden gasp had come from him. Slowly, she had moved closer towards his body, again another gasp.

Her pulse had still been racing as reminders of all the abuse, the violence, the hurt she had endured swept over her at the realization that, after all these years, there was her husband lying in a defenceless heap, at her mercy. It was now or never. Instinct had taken over. She had pulled the handkerchief from her pocket then pushed it into his open mouth with her fingers, down towards his throat, forcing it as far as the cloth would go.

Falling backwards against the wall she had waited, adrenaline pumping through her. Sweat had run down her grimy face. It had seemed to go on forever … a static scene, not a sound. No motion had come from the body; it was lifeless.

Her eyes had now accustomed to the dim light and it was with a fearful frenzy of survival, without a plan in mind, that she had started to shovel the heap of coal to one side. Her strength: a defiance, a release.

It must have taken her half an hour to move the coal and drag his body across the floor, positioning it under the manhole shoot, and then shovelling the coal back in place covering the body. She had been sure to remove the hanky from his throat.

Her breathing had steadied by now as she looked at the coal heap, assuring herself it looked as it did before, after it had been delivered.

But she had been shivering as she finally climbed up the stairs from the cellar. Once in the kitchen, she had turned, closed the cellar door, and locked it.

Upstairs she had run a hot bath, undressed then stepped into it; lowering herself down. Gradually, the shivering had subsided and she had lain back in the clean hot water, as it enveloped her body and calmed her mind.

She had remained in the bath for a good twenty minutes before she started to consider what she had done - trying to rationalise, putting her plans in place. Finally, she had decided that she would go straight to the police station first thing in the morning.

After the bath she had dressed ready for bed, then put the coal-stained clothes into the water and washed them.

That night had not been for sleeping as she had started to judge her actions. It occurred to her as she lay there that, from her past experiences, had the events in the cellar not happened as they did, by now she would have been nursing an injury from another brutish attack. Now there was no pain in her body. Even if it meant prison, that would be better than all the fear and pain.

At some time in the early hours, she must have dozed off to sleep because the next thing she remembered was waking with a start as daylight came in the bedroom and with it the reality of what she had done had come flooding back.

She had got up, prepared to go straight to the police station and ready to tell them the whole story. By the time she was washed and dressed, she felt positive about what she was going to do. Standing in front of the mirror, she had composed herself.

Coming out of the house, closing the door behind her, she had felt the cold morning air on her face and set off walking. Everything had seemed so normal outside; how could that be?

Puzzling over this, she'd walked towards the end of the street passing the pub on the corner and, to her surprise, there had been workmen boarding up the windows. A **Property For Redevelopment** sign was being fixed to the wall of the building.

What was going to happen now the pub was

closed? Where would the locals drink? Of course, they would be split up, going to other pubs elsewhere in the neighbourhood. This would mean his mates would be drinking at different pubs.

The more she had walked on, the more the thought grew in her mind: who would ask where he was? Would anyone? She knew there had been rumours that he was very friendly with the bar maid and that she had been thinking of leaving the area. The woman must have known the pub was going to be closing.

Something triggered inside her head, was she doing the right thing by going to the police? Maybe she should wait and see what happened; everything was changing. All of a sudden, she had found herself turning round, walking back home. She would just sit tight.

The weekend had passed, nobody had queried his whereabouts. Monday came; at midday his works phoned to enquire where he was, saying that he hadn't turned up that morning. Without hesitating, she had told them that she had not seen him since Friday and mentioned how worried she was. They had agreed that she should report it to the police.

Again, she relived the following Tuesday morning. Standing outside the police station. taking a deep breath before she walked up the steps. Going through the main door, she had slowly made her way towards the desk. A man was already standing at the desk, talking to the duty sergeant, and she couldn't help overhearing their conversation. The man was reporting a missing dog, and was giving the policeman the details, after which the sergeant replied:

'Yes sir, we will let you know if we hear anything.'

'Thank you.' said the man, and departed.

She had stood there uncertain, thinking: *should she just walk back out*.

'Can I help you, madam?' asked the sergeant, waking her from her trance. 'Eh pardon, madam, can I help you?'

'Well,' she had said, moving nearer to the desk. 'I don't know what to say only …' Then just blurting out: 'It's my husband … he hasn't come home.'

'What do you mean?' the policeman asked.

As she answered, the words just came pouring out. 'I haven't seen my husband since Friday morning and I've no idea where he is. He went to work on Friday morning and hasn't returned.'

'Can you think of any reason why he may not have come home madam?' the sergeant asked in a soft comforting voice.

He had led her through all the details of his description, getting her to reiterate what she knew regarding her husband's movements as to his usual routine, and how he had always gone to the pub straight after work on a Friday evening. She also mentioned the phone call from his boss the previous morning, about him not being at work. Admitting that she had not really known his work or social friends and also hinting at the rumours regarding the bar maid.

At the end of her statement, the sergeant said: 'Look, madam, I'm sorry but we can't do much straight away as it's only been a few days. But we will send a WPC round to see you before the end of the week. Let us know if you hear anything, or if he returns in the meantime. Feel free to call us any time.' He finished, handing her a card with the local telephone inquiry line number.

She had walked away from the station into the sunshine in a daze. How had she managed to say all that and not mention that her husband was lying dead in the cellar? How and why had she not told the truth? She almost couldn't believe it herself. All the same, felt like a weight off her mind. With the warmth of the sun on her face she had decided that whatever happened, things were going to be different.

Through the week that followed there were a couple of enquiries from locals and neighbours. Her answer had been that she had no idea of his whereabouts, had told the police and they were still looking. Everyone had been sympathetic and wished her well.

As promised, at the end of the week, a women constable turned up at her front door. She said she had come to report on the progress of their inquiries so far, and that they had not been able to come up with any information regarding her husband's disappearance. The constable asked if she could come in to see if there was anything in his belongings that might help with their inquiries.

After going around the house, they sat down in the lounge drinking a cup of tea.

'Now, we have located and spoken to some of his friends,' said the WPC,' and a couple of them said they remember him at the pub last Friday evening. Your husband had been drinking as usual. He had been tanked up, as they put it, when he left. They also mentioned the barmaid had finished early, saying she had a train to catch and had a taxi waiting. They also mentioned she was especially fond of your husband and he used to joke that one day he'd run away with her.' The policewoman flashed a glance at her to see how she was taking this information before going on. 'We can try and follow up on this lady's whereabouts, but you must realise we would not be at liberty to disclose where he is, or indeed if he is with this woman, unless he wishes. I don't want to build up your hopes, but when people go off at his time of life it usually means they don't want to be found. You have told me he wasn't ill or anything, and we have checked out the hospitals for admissions.'

This said, she assured her that all the necessary procedures would be put in place, that he would be added to their circulated missing persons list and that details would be distributed between all area police forces.

Inevitably, the inquiries led to no results and she had become almost in denial as to what happened. She had never had reason to unlock the cellar door and since that Friday night her life had continued. She had become confident, and self-sufficient, getting herself a job in town, and making new friends.

As the years passed most of the inhabitants of streets in the area had been re-housed, moving out in phases. Now it was the turn of the remaining residents who were mostly elderly or single people. Soon the developers were moving in, knocking down, and clearing all the rows of terraced houses in that area, including the pub on the corner. They said the bulldozers would be arriving within the next two weeks. Shortly, she would be moving into a brand new flat on the Princes Estate, with all mod cons and would be able to take her cat with her. A pleasurable feeling came over her, another new chapter in her life.

The packing of her belongings had already started. Having taken next week as leave from work it meant she would be able to move into her new home by the next weekend. Tomorrow she would start getting the rest of the packing done; the removal van would be arriving on Thursday morning.

Sitting in the arm chair she snuggled herself down, with the television on, the cat settled on her lap. All doors and windows closed tight and curtains drawn. Contented, she felt everything was going to work out fine. She sat there feeling the warmth of the gas fire against the front of her legs. Gradually, she began to drift off, her eyes slowly closing, her breathing steady, she fell into a deep sleep.

It was Thursday midday when the police broke down the back door. All was silent inside the house. The constable opened the door into the sitting room. There she was still sitting in the arm chair with the cat on her lap.

At the coroner's inquiry the pathologist's report confirmed the cause of death and it was read out.

Asphyxiation due to carbon monoxide poisoning.

The engineer's report stated that the lack of servicing over many years had caused the gas fire to malfunction.

Autumn Fair

To the years that have passed, some joy, some sorrow
This regular season comes without fail
The golden sun projecting its rays on this pallet of
colour
Too varied for the eye to count,

Now the leaves have started to fall,
Making a carpet for the children to run through
Kicking them in the air, joy, laughter
Fulfilling as their time is now

Look around, this is nature's autumn fair
Spread out before you, following the same pattern
As to the clock we can never stop
Our lives move on whatever,

In anticipation, less as age progresses
knowing the inevitable death that comes at the end
So enjoy, live this life to the full
The rewards are all in the mind to savour,
with all your senses.

Lizzy

The Visit

They say never go back, but Lizzy had taken the opportunity to do so.

Here she was in Henny Back Lane, a hamlet which consisted of just three dwellings. Looking down the overgrown path towards what had once been her family home all those years ago, her heart sank. It was no longer the little picturesque white pebble-dash bungalow with its red-slated roof. The windows had been bricked up and a corrugated tin roof installed; it looked as if it was now being used as a storage shed.

She found it hard to recall what it had been like all those years ago living here, with their very basic way of life, but full of happy times. The building lay way back from the road, set in a large plot of land; you could describe as a small field. The nearest neighbours then were the Gallespies they had lived about two hundred yards up the road to the right - Ansells Farm, which was and still is a large impressive house with white wicket fencing around the front. Mr Gallespie had been an ex-colonial army officer who married an Indian lady and they had one son, Tom. The other dwelling, some five hundred yards to the left, was an old thatch cottage which also looked surprisingly well maintained. In those days, it was a youngish couple, Ron and Connie who lived there after the war.

Even the old pond opposite, utilised then, was now overgrown to half its original size. She suddenly remembered when her children, Mary and Leslie, used to catch the baby moorhens and put them in the large tin bath to paddle about in along with newts, and frogspawn had a large glass bowl to develop and swim around.

All these snippets of memories started to return.

It was following her marriage to Alf in London where they were both born. Mary had been about a year old by then, and with the outbreak of war looming it was time to take a gamble and move out to the countryside. So, they settled in Suffolk purchasing this as a smallholding of forty-four acres. For Alf it was a challenge; Lizzy realised after that her savvy streetwise city dweller husband was no farmer. It was a steep learning curve for both of them. Even so they managed and were away from all the tensions to the build up to WW11. She smiled, recalling some of the trials and tribulations they went through during that time ... if nothing else they had the good fresh air and enjoyed the beautiful countryside surrounding them away from all that city noise and smog, and being somewhat self-sufficient. By 1941, their farming hopes were dashed, (but in retrospect it had been a godsend) as the land was taken over for the war effort.

It was January 1942 when their son Leslie was born, but by the May that year Alf had been called up to the army. Then came the hard slog of holding everything together.

Looking back, she wondered how they got through those wartime years, with all the uncertainty along with everyone else. There had been a couple of times Alf came home briefly on leave before he was sent overseas.

Her heart rose remembering that day in 1946, that afternoon when the one and only taxi in the village of Alphamstone arrived at the bottom of the path in the lane. How she'd seen Alf in his army uniform as he climbed out followed by Mary who he had picked up from school. Then with haversack slung over his shoulder and carrying a suitcase he'd walked up the path towards the front door. She savoured the moment when she had dropped everything, had felt as though she was flying as she ran to meet them. Their embrace was so tight; she knew that from then on all would be well and nothing else mattered. The family was complete and now they would rebuild their lives together.

Following a lovely sunny holiday by the sea, Alf was lucky - he managed to get a job which was only half a mile down the lane. An American company had started up at the local sandpit works making concrete coloured brick. This being a full-time steady job, it was easy to rent the land out as it was good quality agricultural land. Over the coming year they made a lovely home of the bungalow doing all sort of improvements. There was no running water apart from an ingenious system Alf rigged with forty gallon drums as rain butts on each corner of the bungalow at various levels, so by inter-connecting pipes to each one in turn then to a tap over the Belfast sink, their drinking water was carried in a pail from a pump. They'd had no electric power, just log fires to heat and a cast iron range to cook, along with paraffin lamps and candles to light the dark nights. There'd been a large tin bath to bathe in, and of course the toilet was something else. A wooden TARDIS that stood in the back yard along with a galvanised bucket, a wooden bench with a hole and a supply of newspaper cut into squares on a string.

She was still finding it hard to imagine what had gone before looking around the place. All the pleasures and rewards they had worked for, all the wonderful produce from their orchard with its glut of fruit to eat, cook, and preserve. Those gardens full with the seasonal flowers and vegetables so tasty, as well as the fresh eggs, chickens, rabbits, and, even then, the twice delivery service butcher and baker. All those predictable seasons of boiling hot summers and snow every winter; you could set your clock to them. The winters so cold, wakening with ice on the inside of the windows. She had been so fit in those days walking the children to school three miles and back twice a day in their early years. Always enjoying her surrounding during those days.

There was never much money but life was full and wholesome, so good for the children in so many ways. Never bored, making our entertainment apart from a weekly trip on the bus to the market town of Sudbury for a bit of shopping and treats, fish and chips, then to the cinema, followed by a late evening trip home.

Their lives then followed on with Mary getting married and with her two sons later settling in South Africa and Leslie going off to sea in the Merchant Navy.

With a sigh she left Henny Back Lane behind her as she headed towards the village, cutting over the fields following the footpath leading down to where the stile gave access to the path that leads up through the chase. This stretch was especially wonderful at this time of the year. The trees overhanging, making a covered tunnel which sloped up towards the village, it was Autumn with a kaleidoscope of colour and the positioning of this parallel line of the trees facing south-west with the late afternoon sun low in the sky a distant glow giving an almost mystical atmosphere. Coming out at the end, it opened out to a view of the triangular village green, with the village hall running along the top side. Alphamstone was always a place of activity with the fairs, functions, and dances, in those day. Everyone knew everyone and help and advice was always available. One shop had been owned by the Butlers – Mr & Mrs and two children - the man with the taxi.

Lizzy could remember them all, names and addresses passing by their homes. The Harrings, Stucks, Parkers ... the Harrings, yes, she thought she could go on and on. Passing all these dwellings, acknowledging that was in her past. Now ... who knows? She was now at the bottom edge of the village where the road forks with the main road to the right sloping off downhill to Lamarsh then on to Bures.

There in front of her was the village Church. This ancient building with its wooden spire. It had been said the Roundheads stabled their horses in it during the Civil War. Lizzy was now in amongst the gravestones, pleased to see the area has been kept up together. It's been a long, long, long time; she passed stones with familiar names. It is here somewhere. Yes, there it is; it's obvious no one has been to tend it in the years that have passed. You can just make out the names there, just still visible under the lichen and weathering.

I'm so glad I was allowed to come back, she thought to herself looking at the memorial stone and thinking of her Alf. *We will always be together.*

REST IN PEACE
HERE LIES
ALFRED HERBERT HENSON
AND
ELIZABETH QUEENIE HENSON
A BELOVED WIFE AND MOTHER

Dead Timing

It was only 2.30 in the afternoon but seemed much later in the day as the sun hung low in the November sky. All she could think of was those wonderful days spent in the garden during the summer, now, that was at an end. With a cool breeze now blowing from the west she decided to go indoors.

Kim, the dog, followed as she walked to the shed to put away the shears; upon opening the door, she noticed that some of the garden equipment had been disturbed. Bending forward to pick up the tarpaulin that had fallen to the floor she drew it up towards her, then startled, jumped back. There was a pair of legs poking out from underneath. Holding her breath she drew the tarpaulin back further, in doing so gradually started to reveal the rest of a body. It was recognisable to her straight away, it was the next-door neighbour's cat, and it was dead.

"It's poor Tiger!" she whispered, looking at the dog.

Kim responded with a vacant look, showing a complete lack of interest. Without any doubt, if that cat *had* been alive, he would have been chasing its ass off around the garden. Still talking to the dog she said: "I'll have to go and tell poor old Gladys now." Again, from Kim there was no reaction.

A little later she was at Glady's front door, which was two doors down the road. Using the knocker and also pressing the bell to make sure the elderly lady would hear. After repeating this motion several times, she gave up. Then turning to leave, she saw a woman she knew, the next-door neighbour down unloading her car with some shopping.

She called out: "Hello I've just been trying to call on Gladys, but there's no reply."

"I haven't seen her for a couple of days now, she usually phones to let me know if she'd like anything from the shops," said the woman. Then the woman carried on saying: "I'll get Tom to go round to see if she's okay, he'll be home soon. He's got a key."

Two hours later, dark now outside, she glanced though her front window, as the blue flashing light brightened the road. She noticed an ambulance and a police car outside Gladys' house.

Putting a coat over her shoulders she went out to see what was happening, she could see Tom at the front gate of the old lady's house. "Tom, is there a problem with Gladys?" she asked as she approached him.

"Yes, I'm afraid so, Gladys is dead. They say it looks like natural causes."

"Oh no! what a shame!" she said "I tried knocking earlier to tell her that her cat was dead"

As she walked back into her home, she just could not believe it.

Going through to the kitchen, she looked down at Kim in his basket, and speaking directly to him,

"It's poor old Gladys ... she's died, how sad that should happen."

Kim looked up at her briefly, then just snuggled his head down and closed his eyes.

Ruth

Period Return

Keynsham Railway Station, 2010

Ruth boarded the 11.56 train to Weymouth with some apprehension. By the time she had stowed her weekend case and settled into a forward-facing window seat, she felt comfortable with herself. As the train pulled out of the station, her feelings once more reverted to the anticipation that had been dominating her thoughts all week. She was going to meet Robert, the man she had been in love with some thirty years ago, whose memories she still held close.

Bath Spa Station

The train, after stopping at Bath where it disgorged a large proportion of its passengers, then proceeded. It was, she knew, scheduled to stop at every station along the way, until the final destination. The train started its climb out of Bath and, as the journey progressed, she was able to enjoy the scenery, taking in the views across the city. It was autumn now and apart from the few evergreens, the trees and foliage were on the change, their leafed canopies glowing in the midday sun which enhanced the kaleidoscope of glorious shades of gold, red, and yellow.

Freshford Station

In her handbag was a photo of the man she had known in years gone by. It showed a tall blond-haired man; she remembered his abundant energy, his blue eyes and the gazes they had shared. Their love had been real, so full and deep. They had spent so much time together.

She had been a nursing sister in a London hospital; she loved her job, enjoying the position that she had worked hard to attain. He was a trainee surgeon already making his mark. They had met during a get-together with mutual friends. It all seemed to click on that first date. They had talked and talked with no sense of time and from then on they were inseparable when not working. Later, they had moved into a flat together and, as time passed, they spoke of getting married, making plans for their future life together.

Avoncliff Station

Her eyes staring unseeing out of the train window, she recalled how it had all changed. They had just arrived back in London after their holiday in Cornwall. They had hired a cottage for a week, their time spent enjoying each other. She remembered the long walks on the beach when, acting in childlike fashion, they had run in and out of the surf, and the delicious pub lunches with fresh sea food. Those wonderful evenings just listening to the radio with the lights low, sipping wine by the open fire, when they would make love. She had missed that intimacy so much, that love and warmth in her life.

Bradford-on-Avon Station

Things had started falling apart following the phone call from her sister that evening back at their flat. It had been bad news: their father had died and the funeral was on the following Saturday. She remembered how saddened she had been, considering both parents had given so much to her and her sister. Not only with their love but by their own sacrifices, providing both daughters with the opportunity to have a good education. Such a fulfilled family life; they could not have asked for more. She recalled her surprise that it had been her father who had died and not her mother. She had been the one with ill health, not him. In fact, over the previous four years her father had been stalwart in looking after his wife as she needed constant care. They had still managed to have a happy, yet somewhat restricted life together.

Trowbridge Station

On the Saturday, she and Robert had travelled to Keynsham on the train to attend the funeral. Everything had gone well; her sister had arranged everything beautifully. Following the gathering afterwards, she had conferred with her sister as they needed to arrange things regarding mum. It was decided it would be best if Ruth took some leave, staying on to help sort things out. Her sister would be able to stay for a while, but needed to return to Birmingham soon to get back to her husband and two young children.

Their parents lived in the same small cottage on the edge of the town where they had raised their children. The cottage was surrounded by a good-sized garden which had become overgrown as their father was unable to cope, his time taken up with their mother's care.

Westbury Station

The track flattened out and the train started to gather speed between the various stops, as more passengers were hopping on and off. Ruth sat comfortably enjoying the warmth of the sun coming through the window. *If only things had turned out differently*, she sighed.

Looking back, she could see that it was just the reality of the situation then. She *had* tried; had it been loyalty, or just a conscious sense of duty returning an outstanding debt of gratitude? *You cannot live your life with regret*, she thought. Maybe nowadays it could have been arranged differently, who knows.

It was only now, nine months since mother had died, that she was realising that she had lived these past years of her life around her mother's needs, and just made the best of her situation.

Frome Station

During the days following their father's funeral, they had first to sort out his Will and affairs, then came the discussions about the situation regarding mother's care. Father had made tentative provision with his pension plus a small life insurance but, due to inflation, that was never going to be enough to pay for full time carers. Ruth respected the fact that her sister would only be able to do so much as her situation was different.

They had talked to Mum about going into a care home - an option she did not relish, as her mental state was still good and she was very aware of her surroundings. So, they then considered live-in care which might work well. Ruth knew her sister wouldn't be in a position to contribute much towards the cost, so it would be down to her. They even tried to raise a loan against the cottage, as their parents owned the freehold but, in the end, this proved to be not viable.

Eventually her sister went home to Birmingham and Ruth stayed on to settle the live-in care, also to see how the initial cost could be covered. She had savings put by, money saved for her previous wedding plans, and by adding in the small endowment their father had left, she knew they would be able cope in the short term. However, as time went on, she had to extend her compassionate leave and Robert had taken to coming down some weekends. They'd thought that things would eventually work out. Unfortunately, the live-in home care did not work. Mother felt it was an encroachment on her way of life having someone living in the house and she was not at ease with the fact that communication with the carer was difficult. She had become more and more reliant on Ruth who spent a considerable amount of time and effort explaining that she would have to go back to her job in London, otherwise she could lose it.

Bruton Station

Then came the phone call from Robert. He had been offered the opportunity to work in America on a two-year internship at a prestigious hospital. Naturally, he did not want to miss this opportunity. Equally naturally he wanted her to go with him. In fact, he had already made inquiries with regard to obtaining visas for them both, so she would have no trouble getting work. The pay would be to both their advantage, which would help towards their future plans.

She had told him she would have to think about it, as she still hadn't managed to get her mum settled. He agreed; the job wasn't until September, so that gave them three months to sort things out. Anyway, he was coming to Keynsham that weekend, so they would be able to discuss the situation. It had all sounded very exciting.

That weekend they had discussed the situation and decided that Robert should go to America first, and get settled then she could follow after Christmas, by which time things should be sorted. She knew her mother was deteriorating health-wise and had thought that she *would*, though reluctantly, be persuaded to go into a nursing home. The finances would work, she decided, working on the assumption that she would be earning a higher income by working abroad. Financially it could work out and her mother would be in good care. She could then have periodic trips back home. It was all settled. Also, her sister could come down to visit from time to time as her children became less dependent.

Castle Cary Station

The week before Robert was due to leave, her sister came down to stay at the cottage in Keynsham so Robert and Ruth could spend some time together in London.

After that, they wrote frequently. Robert's letters were full of how much he liked working in America, and how he was sure that she would love it. There were so many opportunities.

Although Ruth was still having problems getting things sorted for her mother, she was sure it would work out. In her letters to Robert, she had kept saying how much she was looking forward to joining him.

Yeovil Pen Mill Station

Christmas came. Robert had leave and managed to fly home. It had been such a lovely treat for them both. Naturally, he was expecting her to return with him but she was still under pressure as she had not managed to settle her mother, mainly because she had not had any luck finding a good nursing home. Some proved to have unsuitable conditions, where you would not want to leave a loved one and others, at the opposite end of the spectrum, were like a five-star hotel where the costs were prohibitive.

They had tried to move Mother to a home nearer to her sister, which would make things easier, but to no avail. It just seemed that there was an absence of the right sort of place, the sort of place that would be best for Mother.

She could sense the resentment growing in Robert as the time drew near for him to return to America. She had tried to convince him it would only be a few more months. After New Year's Eve he was ready to leave.

She recalled that moment, those feelings of gloom and disappointment in herself, as they said their goodbyes. That sadness between them, remembering it showed in his eyes as they had parted, and how she had promised that she would make things work for them. Despite all the problems, she had been determined to overcome this stumbling block. She had cried, feeling bitter that their love was drifting apart.

They had still exchanged letters but as time went on these became less frequent. By the autumn of that year communication had almost stopped. They had both realised it wasn't going to work.

Eventually securing some home help enabled Ruth to work part-time at the Bath hospital, which had helped with the finances. Her sister had contributed where possible. The cottage over the years had been brought up to date; Ruth enjoyed learning D.I.Y along the way. Also, the garden had taken her interest and become one of her major hobbies; she took a pride in her achievements. She also had a dog now, the company of which she loved. They took walks in the park which made her get out into the fresh air, and she enjoyed daily chats with fellow walkers.

Thornford Station

At the end of the two years, Robert had returned to the UK. Ruth then heard from a mutual friend that he had arrived home with a lady, an American. The friend also informed her that she had heard they were planning to get married in the spring.

Through the years that followed she had been kept up to date on his activities: his career, eventual marriage and subsequent family, his moving into a select suburb of London.

Later, as the years passed the flow of information ceased and she just got on with her life. During this period, she had had a platonic relationship with a married man, but knew it was going nowhere. Not that she wanted anything else due to her circumstances, which still hadn't changed. She was living a life to which she was now resigned, taking comfort from the fact that her mother was getting the best possible care.

Yetminster Station

As the train pulled away from the station, she observed that the seats around her were empty. She'd been so lost in her memories that she had not noticed. Opening her bag, she took out the old photo of Robert and tenderly stroked the picture with her thumb. It was the picture she normally kept in the drawer of her dressing table along with his letters. From time to time, she would take it out and reminisce of the times they had shared together. What a handsome guy he had been. The photograph had been taken on a trip they had made to the Avebury Stone Circles and he was shown posing in front of one of the enormous stones. Her heart warmed to think he had been hers, the love they'd shared which had been lost, but never completely died.

Chetnole Station

She had only seen Robert once after his marriage. It must have been about four years afterwards. She cast her mind back, it had been at a friend's wedding. She had gone, not realising Robert would be there. The church has been quite full when she entered, she remembered, and she hadn't noticed him in the crowd. Later at the reception whilst talking to some old acquaintances, she happened to look up and had spotted him. The woman, presumably his wife, standing next to him looked nice and was beautifully groomed. He also looked smart though she thought he had put on a bit of weight - due to life's contentment no doubt?

He had looked in her direction and, for a moment, it seemed as though he was going to come across the room toward her. But she had panicked, made excuses to her immediate company, and hurried off to the Ladies.

She had stayed there more than fifteen minutes, her heart racing; she felt so awkward, embarrassed. Why? Oh, why? Couldn't she have put on a brave face and just talked to him? It would have been the adult thing to do.

Eventually finding some courage and opening the door cautiously, she had found the nearest exit and taken herself outside where she took some deep breaths to steady herself. Then she'd caught the bus to the train station, for home. Travelling home, she had sadly realised that meeting him would not have made any difference to the situation, only raise old regrets.

Maiden Newton Station

She now reminded herself why she was undertaking this journey. It had been about two and a half weeks ago, on the Wednesday when, on returning from Bath, she had picked up the mail from the door mat. To her surprise there had been a hand-written envelope addressed to her. On opening she had realised straight away it was from Robert, although the handwriting was a little scrawled. *Dear Ruth*, he had written, *I hope you are well.* He had apologised for writing if it was inappropriate, not knowing her circumstances. Reading on, she learned that he had been living in Weymouth for six years since retiring. He had originally moved there with his wife, Mandy, then she had contracted terminal cancer and sadly passed away two and a half years ago. Although he liked living in Weymouth, he felt isolated from most of his past friends and was thinking of going back to London to be near his son. The son was now married and living with his wife and two daughters in Robert's old house. She read that the son was now a medical professional, becoming an anaesthetist, and working at the same hospital where they had both previously worked. She smiled at the coincidence.

He went on by reiterating that he hoped his getting in touch had not offended her in any way, and would understand if she declined his wish to make contact. At the end he had wished her well for the future, saying that he would like to keep in touch if possible and adding his email address at the bottom.

After a couple of days, she had plucked up enough courage to respond by email. Twenty-four hours later she had had a reply. From then on, the emails had flowed almost daily and eventually the content had turned to reminiscing, referring to the things they had done together, remembering the old times. She found she started to check her emails with anticipation, sensing a tingle in her being and she felt herself smiling a lot for no obvious reason. There was no way she could blame him for what had happened in the past.

It was Ruth that had initiated the idea for them meeting up. She would travel to Weymouth and now she was doing just that. The date had been set.

Dorchester West Station

She glanced at her wristwatch, another twenty-five minutes and she would be at Weymouth. Her excitement began to build along with anticipation. Here she was at sixty years of age, feeling like a teenager! What was she expecting to come of all this? So much of her life had changed since they last met, *water under the bridge*. It had been thirty years; was this to be the new life she was looking for? In that moment, she felt she just wanted to hold him close to her and say nothing. She couldn't blame him for what had gone before. Is this the chance she wants to take?

She hadn't even met him yet and there she was making plans. Try to think sensibly. She told herself. But it was hopeless, the nearer she got to her destination the more she started to fantasise.

Bringing a weekend bag and booking a room at the Royal Hotel, that wasn't too forward, was it? Ruth, you don't have to justify your actions. You are allowed to have a break. You're just meeting an old friend at the seaside.

She turned her attention to the world outside the train window in an effort to calm herself. Along the route she'd noticed the upkeep of some of the stations. Now, looking at the pretty flower pots, and hanging baskets she saw that the plants were now at the end of their final blooming before the approach of winter. Almost holding on to what they have; making the most of life, not just giving up while there's a chance to live. The autumn of life, before the inevitable.

Upway Station

Opening her handbag again she took out a small mirror, checked her face and touched up her make up. Not that she had ever worn much; she felt confident now and not too overdressed despite the fact she had taken all of two hours that morning to get ready. After showering, she had stood in front of the mirror changing into one outfit, then another. Totally incapable of being able to make up her mind. She so much wanted to make a good impression, knowing it was silly, but she still had that image of his wife, so elegant looking at that wedding reception.

Eventually she had settled for smart casual and packed a light shower-proof top coat with some sensible shoes in case they decided to walk along the beach.

The train was starting to slow now, within a few minutes it would be arriving at Weymouth Station, most people were starting to organise themselves, collecting their belongings.

Weymouth Station

Now that the train was pulling into the platform her heart rate started to increase. After all this time she just could not wait. After an eternity, the train stopped. A great movement of bodies was now taking place as passengers and luggage evacuated the carriages.

Reaching up, she pulled down her case; it was only light so she could carry it easily. Ruth alighted from the carriage, becoming part of the mass exodus swarming towards the platform end. She had felt comfortable bringing the overnight case, but did not want to seem presumptuous at their meeting so, finding a station locker, she stowed the case, putting the key safely in her handbag.

Once out of the station, she walked up the road towards the sea front. Her pace quickened along with her heart rate. She knew she had to turn left at the top, at the road junction, to reach the clock tower where they had arranged to meet. The excitement started to grow inside her. What would her reaction be when they met? After all that time spent caring for her mother. This was *her* time now!

As she walked towards the clock tower, she noticed the time, the train must have been early, as it was only 1.56. Perhaps he hadn't arrived yet. People were walking past in both directions.

She spread her gaze, looking across the wide promenade towards the sea. There in front of the promenade rail she could make out a tall figure sitting on a bench seat facing out to sea.

Could it be Robert?

Quickening her pace, she walked across the promenade towards the seafront. As she approached the bench, she was sure, yes it *was* him.

Then just a few steps away, almost there, she slowed her pace. "Robert?"

She felt her voice crack as she said his name. He turned his head towards her, looking up with a smile; but his face was old, just recognisable, showing the visible signs of a stroke.

"Robert." She spoke again, not able to restrain the shock mixed with overwhelming disappointment which showed in her voice as her heart sank. He was not sitting on the bench, as she had thought, instead he was sat in a wheelchair.

Halloween

October's laast day, when long dark shadows fall
As of timed tradition the spirits call
Ghosts, and ghouls come on the scene
For tonight's the night of Halloween!

Hurrying home, this dark night comes alive,
From flitting bats you cower, as they duck and dive
Wavering branches rustle against flickering street
light
The hooting owl, as the imagination take fright,

Pumpkins lined up along stone wall
Scooped out, carved with sharpened tool
Candles lit, placed within their shell
Project their illuminated spooky masks of hell

See silhouetted against the moonlit sky
With pointed hat, her billowing cape lets fly
Black cat hunched, rides the witch's broom
As light reflects her hideous face of doom

Sounds caught upon, as sharp winds blow
when the werewolf howls, its fear to sow.
Hear wailing sounds of un-rested souls,
Are we safe this night, as the death bell tolls

Hear those sounds out in the dark, puts mind to
scatter
Skulls that chatter, headless riders horse clatter
While the spider weaves its silken web,
to catch its victims, until they're dead

Are we safe down in our bed,
by pulling the covers overhead.
Be brave, fear not, just hold on till the dawn
When you'll laugh at yourself, as a new day is born

Then comes that dreaded knock, upon your very door,
open up, see there before you, a sight of gruesome
gore,
Yes! They've come for *you!* Now there is no retreat
You only have just one of two choices, ***Trick or Treat***

Two Minutes Silence

A collective act: an individual moment.

Thoughts and feelings

It was during this silent time I realised the answer to a question that I had been pondering for some time,

At my age whom do you thank for such a good life, in this mixed-up world. Naturally I thank my late parents, my family and friends, but also this country I've grown up in.

A life fashioned without any great hardship and been lucky to embrace that laid before me.

Good times bad times have come and gone, but I've been lucky enough to be in an environment where solutions are possible,

to be able to survive without threat nor favour of some power being placed upon me.

In that silence I realised the reason for that freedom given, it was because of all those people before and present that had given lives and pain in duty defending Britain and making it the country it is today, we must always remember and be thankful.

Netsuke

Objects of beauty laid before me
Of ivory and bone, wood and stone
Sculptures imagination inspired
A guided hand to carve, and hone

A Heritage of Japanese tradition
Small yet so defined, form within form
Used for purpose, from bygone years
Kimono sash placed, objects to adorn

A cherished form there portrayed,
Its image to please, its time to last
Mystic formed figures held within
As heirlooms have been passed

Delicate shapes the eye perceives
Fingers follow each twist and fold
Soft in form, yet hard with touch
Holds meanings, a story to be told

Recollections 2020

It was mid-afternoon. Outside, a cold overcast drizzly day. I sat in a window-seat, looking out through the window panes of an old Georgian building at Gallery 44AD. The view diagonally across the street, dominated by Bath Abbey. This iconic building, with its weathered, aged, stone bulk, situated at the far side of the square. Its reflection spread out across the wet flagstones before it, while its blackened architectural Gothic towers reached up, piercing the dull grey, clouded skies.

The Gallery is situated on the corner of the street. Constructed of Bath stone, it had originally been a house consisting of three floors and a basement but now stripped bare, with its white wall creating a light space but still retaining the old fireplaces as a feature, the gallery display area occupying two of the floors plus basement.

I had come here that afternoon to meet Joe, an art associate, company while he was doing his shared stewarding for the gallery. Joe had had one of his artworks selected for the exhibition - theme: Material World. Being a painter myself I had enjoyed looking around the exhibits. Most of the artwork was of a very contemporary nature, probing one's mind against the titles, a challenge in itself prompting, no doubt, conflicting opinions in the viewers.

We had been there since midday and been with our own company most of the time, the low attendance no doubt this being due to the inclement weather. Various visitors had come and gone in dribs and drabs, it was interesting hearing their points of view and comments. A couple of the other exhibiting artists had also been in to have a chat, as artists do.

As the afternoon slowly progressed, I looked up from my position in the gallery and noticed a lady stepping over the threshold of the main doorway. She was of mature year, of medium height, and dressed in dark clothes, appropriate to weather. Her attire was not run of the mill - instead she had a style that stood apart, definitely her own person. She walked about the gallery for some time, ending up in what was the main room. Joe struck up a conversation with her; his own artwork hung on the rear wall nearby. They were both involved, speaking at length regarding conception and construction of the work.

In joining the discussion, I noticed the lady had a kind face full of character, together with soft blue eyes, which held a sparkle. This is something I tend to notice, being aware of faces, I like painting portraiture. From the way she spoke, I deduced the lady had a great interest in the subject matter of art and asked if she was an artist herself. In replying to my question, she said, she was not, but told me that she was a writer.

I was immediately greatly interested in what she said as I had taken up writing myself as a hobby, some ten months previously. I listened to her comments, her voice soft and precise, as she told me that she had been a teacher at George Ward school, Melksham. I could envisage that soft voice being raised to command attention when required. Our conversational subject now progressed onto writing, informing me of a writers' group to which she belonged. Apparently, the group meets up bi-monthly at the Literary and Science Museum in Queen Square, Bath. Seeing my interest, she was kind enough to give me her e-mail address. We also had a short discussion regarding films before leaving. Then we said our goodbyes as she was off to see the newly released film *1917*. As she walked away to mud, blood, and bullets, I thought to myself that it would be a pleasure to see her again at the forthcoming meeting.

On the said day I arrived at Queen Square, like so many places in Bath, it's a wonderful example of Georgian architectural grandeur. The Literary and Science Museum is no exception with its stepped approach to an impressive doorway, opening to a large hallway inside with an ample staircase ascending to the first-floor landing off which was a pair of doors. Going though into a spacious room with large sash windows letting in the daylight, it made an ideal meeting space randomly and modestly furnished with some tables and chairs. On my entering I found the meeting well attended and, on introduction, I was well and truly welcomed to writers and friends from Bath and across the South West area.

It then transpired that the gathering was going to be a meeting in commemoration of the holocaust that took place during the Second World War. Not being aware that was to be the theme of the meeting, I was a bit apprehensive and doubted whether to stay or not.

Then the spokesperson stood and outlined the program for the day's get together. It was going to be a re-enactment of events, offering those who wished a chance to participate in acts and readings related to the holocaust. There was a producer, who was going help organise re-enactments which would be taken from the manuscript of a book that had been written by the lady who had invited me.

The events, covering the time when the Nazis marched in to Vienna and proceeded to round up the Jewish population and subsequently send them to concentration camps in the east, such as those located in Poland. The lady writing the book had done a lot of research and was also a personal victim of the circumstance. As she, along with her family, had been fortunate enough to be evacuated from Vienna before the Nazi occupation.

The idea was we would split into groups and then be given a set of parts which the group would organise between themselves, staging scenes with an arrangement of characters and readers. The first half of the time for rehearsal then, after a midway break, we would act out collectively the complete sequence of the events that had taken place as staged scenarios.

Following a break for lunch during which I enjoyed chatting to the other writers, we arrived at the second half: the imaginary stage was set. This first scene appertained to the Jewish population being told they would need to evacuate their properties and be re-housed somewhere else; they would need to pack as they would be travelling. The Jewish community knew of rumours of the persecution that had been carried out in Germany and became apprehensive to say the least.

The whole of the horrendous scenarios were played out with reading and action from the perpetrated to perpetrators. Emotions were brought to the re-enactment as you could imagine, the stories unfolding with acts and readings so evocative of those times.

One specific scene that for me conjured up the sheer horror of the tragedy that befell these people was where parents were encouraging their young children to pack as if going on holiday, and to take some of their toys and treasured possessions. Also, when the trucks came to take them away it was done under the cover of darkness, so not to arouse too much suspicion in the rest of the population. All were rounded up irrespective of age or abilities. As always it was the rich that had managed to escape, to evacuate themselves from this mass culling which has been shown to be the case in many similar situations before and after in our history.

To me personally, it was a thought-provoking and emotional experience. I hope I am not in any way minimising the Holocaust. This was only one person's eye view of their own place and time, but it has given me a lasting impression of whole Nazi ethos and a pause for thought of how different *our* world would be if the war had taken a different turn.

At the end of the afternoon, I was pleased to have been involved and the whole experience left me with a strong sense that this should never be forgotten and lost in the archives of history. This lesson must be taught to the coming generations so that they realise that true freedom is not given, but something that has been fought for.

The lady who wrote the manuscript went back to Vienna to research her writings which at a later date she was hoping to publish. At the very end she asked those who had attended that, if we felt we wanted to write a piece of work relating the day's events, she would be pleased to put it up on the group website.

I did and these are my feelings in very few words:
Lost property at
the station
Nobody will ever
claim

Trains
traveling
Eastwards
Full of
sorrow, fear
and pain

Touch

An expression in silent relay
Given received, no need to say
A hug or handshake, what does convey
To greet and affirm a pleasure to see
A hand on arm to guide, support kindly

From birth this tactile sense is born
Assurance held in cradled arms warm
This bond as with love takes form
Affections felt, to belong, to care
Becoming family, a longing to share

Emotions of love a touch on the cheek
Just holding hands, no need to speak
Then first kiss, arousal, sensations seek
Uncontrolled feelings, a longing to hold
Becoming one, dreams of pleasures untold

Lost contact of this physical comfort of late
Our need to be close, to confirm and relate
Has brought so much sorrow with heartache
Express sad emotions of grief to for-fill
Lost with no tomorrow a chance to heal

Enveloped in darkness, unable to hear
Our sense of touch is heightened
Reassuring, dispelling loneliness and fear
That simple feeling of touch that says;
It's okay, I'm here

Marjorie

The Red Dress

Marjorie busied herself in the kitchen getting Edward's tea. He would be home soon from golf which he played more often since retiring eighteen months ago. They had thought about downsizing recently, the family-sized home being a detached house in a Thames valley suburb. Their time living there as a family had been enjoyable but now that the children had flown the nest, the house was becoming too big for their requirements, and along with the garden, it was all a bit too much to keep up together.

Marjorie had become very much part of the

local community being involved with the W.I., along with the village fetes, book club, and also singing in a renowned local choir. Edward was still involved with the ex-bankers' association, which included occasional get-togethers.

Now growing old together after their long marriage of contentment, they were very much two peas in a pod. Their rounded stature of similar medium build mirrored each other as a sign of a comfortable living.

It was Autumn time now and Marjorie was looking forward to the choir being able to compete in the National Festival later that month. This year's festival was being held in Northern Ireland; they would be competing against choirs from across the U.K. It was unfortunate the dates had clashed, Edward had other arrangements, he was going to Brighton for his Bankers' Association's annual dinner and get-together during the same week. Otherwise, they would have accompanied each other to their respective events.

Tomorrow, they would be going into town and, hopefully, she would be able to buy the dress she would wear for the competition at the festival. This year's theme co-ordinated colour for the choir was to be red which wasn't to her taste; she felt the colour really didn't suite her,

Ring! Ring! Ring! Ring!

Lifting the receiver to her ear: "Hello" said Marjorie,

"Oh! Hello. Is Eddy there?" the voice on the other end asked.

"Eddy? Are you referring to my husband

Edward?"

"Sorry … is that Mrs Partridge?"

"Yes, it is, to whom am I speaking?"

"It's Jessie from the golf club. I'm just calling to tell you Eddy … I mean Edward … has left his scarf behind."

"Thank you, I will tell him. Good bye." Putting the down receiver abruptly.

That girl sounded rather a bit too familiar in tone, thought Marjorie.

Hearing Edward's car pulling into the driveway she was pleased. As always the tea was prepared, everything laid up ready on the table.

"Hello, my love." said Edward chirpily, as he came through the door.

"I guess you won your game?" Marjorie inquired.

"Yes, we did, actually." he responded boastfully

"I could tell by the tone of your voice" Marjory replied, knowingly. "By the way you had a call - some young woman named Jessie."

"Oh, yes?" replied Edward, looking a bit surprised.

"Apparently she phoned to say you had left your scarf at the club."

"Oh yes, I suppose I must have." He said, realising its absence. "Good of her to phone."

"Seems a lot of trouble for Jessie to go to, being as how you are there again on Thursday, *Eddy*, as *she* called you." she jested in a light-hearted tone.

"Ha! Ha!" Edward replied.

Sitting down for tea, their conversation ran into various subject matter; talk of how the weather was cooling and how the nights were drawing in,

Marjorie's pending choir festival and Edward's convention carried on throughout their meal. The tone of their marriage had always run along these orderly lines everything organised; they disagreed rarely.

In town the next day they both wandered in and out of numerous dress shops. Edward had never resented going with his wife dress hunting, always taking an interest, giving a critical eye and voicing his opinion of what she wore. Marjorie also enjoyed the fact she had a discerning husband and valued his opinion; he had a good eye for colour and style.

She had tried on various red dresses before seeing a style she liked, though she was a bit dubious whether the shade of red would coordinate properly with the rest of the choir for the festival performance.

"Bit bright for you don't you think?" remarked Edward, his face expressing his opinion clearly. He did not approve of it and suggested she should try another shade.

"I know what you mean," she agreed, "it's not my choice of colour at all, but we all have to coordinate."

Marjorie then tried another of a different shade, but still could not make up her mind. After some deliberation, Edward suggested she take both dresses and, if need be, bring one back for refund later.

"Yes, I will do that" Marjorie agreed, as she collected her things and proceeded to the cash desk. After paying they left the store.

Edward drove them home in their car; Marjorie sat in the passenger seat, opening the glove compartment to get a sweet from a packet she usually kept there. As she reached in, she noticed a lipstick tube. Frowning, she withdrew it from the compartment with her forefinger and thumb knowing it was not hers.

"What's this?' She demanded.

"What's what?" Edward asked, keeping his eyes on the road ahead.

"This lipstick in your glove compartment?"

"I don't know. Isn't it yours?"

"I don't think so, it's a ghastly shade of red." She was already inspecting it, taking the top off.

"Well, I've no idea how it got there." Edward, shrugged, now sounding a bit heated.

"Has another woman been in this car?"

Long silence.

"You know Brian and I always go to golf together? Well, I have on an odd occasion dropped Jessie off on our way home. Only because it's on our route."

Edward sounded a bit flustered.

"So what you're saying is it could be hers?" *and what's Brian got to do with it?* she thought.

"*I* don't know, I just answered your question as to whether there had been a woman in the car." He said, trying to stand his ground while concentrating on driving

"Perhaps you can find out when *she* gives you your scarf back on Thursday." She responded in a curt mocking voice.

Thursday: After trying on the two dresses several times in front of the full-length dressing mirror in the corner of the bedroom, she decided eventually on the more subdued shade of red. Marjorie started packing her case. She had felt an air of excitement growing through the week after the choir had their final rehearsal before the pending travel to Northern Ireland.

Friday: At mid-morning the coach arrived to collect Marjorie. As she climbed the step into the coach she could feel and hear the atmosphere of excitement from the choir members already on board. Edward stood at the front gate waving her off with numerous hands reciprocating as the coach pulled away. When the coach had done the rounds collecting all the remaining choir members, it then headed off on route to Holyhead to catch the ferry for the crossing to Dun Laoghaire.

All the choir now sat back to enjoy the trip, and each other's company. As the coach journeyed on, Marjorie was hoping it would be a calm crossing, knowing she wasn't at her best on boats. After about a couple of hours into the journey, the coach pulled into a service station for a comfort stop. All alighted for a chance to stretch their legs. Twenty minutes later, refreshed, they all returned to the coach ready to carry on their journey. It was after the next comfort stop that the coach driver, on checking with his office, came back with bad news. Because of adverse weather conditions, the ferry crossings had been halted until further notice. From then on there were several frantic conversations taking place.

After much deliberation it was agreed, all should return home tonight and, in the meantime, the organisers would try to arrange a flight so they would be able to get to the venue in time to attend the festival. The coach turned for home. The initial disappointment was later dispelled after the trip Organiser announced she had managed to book an early flight from Heathrow. Concluding there would be time to return home and get the flight tomorrow morning all would work out fine.

The coach dropped Marjorie off at the end of the road; it was early evening by now. Although it was only dusk, the lamps down the road were already lit. She thought to herself. *As soon as I get indoors, I'll try and contact Edward, to let him know the situation.* Within five minutes she was at her front door, and was surprised to see the upstairs light was on, Edward must have forgotten to turn it off when he left. Unlocking the front door she stepped into the hallway, the light was filtering down from the upstairs landing. Kicking her shoes off, she walked towards the bottom of the staircase and was a bit startled that she could hear music. She tutted to herself: *I suppose he's left the bedside radio on as well.*

But as she got to the top of the stairs, she could hear movement. Surely a burglar wouldn't put the light on let alone the radio. Her heart was beginning to race. Cautiously with due trepidation, she tiptoed towards the master bedroom. Standing in the doorway, an uncontrollable feeling of growing anger filling her, she stared with amazed eyes at the back of the blond female figure who was swaying to the music in front of *her* full-length mirror … and wearing *her* bloody red dress!

Taking an involuntary deep breath, Marjorie screamed "Edward! where are you?"

Before the sound had stopped echoing around the room, the figure spun around. It was wearing that bright red lipstick and a blond wig. Marjory's jaw dropped in disbelief and disappointment: "Edward?"

Things Without Reason

Things are not always what they seem to be
Complex is our earth's rich pattern
Making it part of life's mystery
Some things in science remain unattainable
Our expectation to conform
Leaving us perplexed or unexplainable
The only fact is a beating heart
Or when time comes and we depart
For we are the caterpillar
That doesn't yet know it's going to be a butterfly

Unconditional Love

1
I'd like to sing the words I've written down
To express the feelings of love, that I've found
My time was going nowhere, my compass unset
Just picking at bare bones, living with a life of regret

2
It was your beauty that touched me when we first met
That moment of meeting I will never forget
You were a light in my darkness, you opened my eyes
There'd be no more cheating no more lies

Chorus
You gave
Unconditional love, no limits to bear
Unconditional love only feelings of care
I know it's for always, I know it's the truth
Unconditional love will always see through

3
You put hope in my soul and love in my heart
Once now together, we would never come to part
Never judging my person or questioned my past
We are loving as soulmates, I know it will last

Chorus

2021

The Vault

Inside the still clinical atmosphere of the bank vault, isolated from the city noise overhead, the only sound breaking the silence was Mr Michael Goldstine as he closed the door of his safety deposit box, followed by the turn of the key locking the compartment door. Temporarily putting the key into the trouser pocket of his Saville Row suit, he stepped back a pace, patted his right hand against his chest with a sense of security for what he had placed within his inside jacket pocket.

Turning to leave, he walked towards the exit; a deep, dull, mechanical thud resonated through the building as the large and heavy vault door before him closed.

'God what's happened?' he asked, directing his comment at the guard by the doorway.

The guard, was already speaking into his short-wave radio. 'Hello! Hello! Unit five to control, what's happened? Over.'

'*Yes!* what has happened?' repeated Goldstine

'Just checking, Sir, there seems to be a problem.' answered the guard.

'Well hurry up I've got business to attend to.' Goldstine was now becoming agitated.

The guard listened intently to his radio then conveying the answer.

'I'm sorry Sir, I've been told the vault has been temporarily closed, due to an incident inside the bank above. They've advised that we stay where we are and police have been called.'

'How long is this going to take?' with an indignant tone.

'Just a moment Sir, I'll check to see.'

Hello control, Hello control, Unit five. Over.' The guard listened for a response.

Radio crackles.

'For ****'s sake what's going on?' Goldstine retorted.

'Sorry, Sir, I'm not getting an answer.'

'What the **** is happening? You mean to say we're stuck here, locked in!' His voice now wavering.

'Yes, Sir, at present. The main thing being if it's any unwanted guests in the bank, then they can't get in here.' The guard answered, his calm voice trying to lighten the atmosphere.

Goldstine fumbled for his mobile. 'I must phone someone.'

'I'm afraid not, Sir, you won't get a signal in here.' The guard informed him with a slow shake of his head.

'This is impossible! Completely unacceptable! Surely *you* must be able to do something!' He was now starting to rant as he paced back and forth

The guard raised his voice in a firm, controlled manner. 'I'll try control again.' he said.

'Isn't there some emergency number you can call on that thing?' Goldstine's voice now becoming pensive. Removing his glasses, he took out his handkerchief and wiped his forehead.

The guard looked at his watch; the time is 1600 hrs.

'We are *not* locked in, it's a safety precaution against whatever problem is going on upstairs, Sir. The exit switch can be activated from inside anytime. As long as the vault door is opened before the timed locking device is activated, it will be all right.' The guard assured him, emphasizing that they could exit any time they wanted before that and that it was just strongly advisable to stay put until it was safe to leave.

'What do you mean the locking device is activated?' Goldstine queried.

'At 1900 hours the lock is activated and the vault remains locked until 0800 hours tomorrow.' Explained the guard patiently.

'*Tomorrow!!*   You must be joking!' retorted Goldstine.

The guard could detect the panic in his voice. 'Please, Sir, I'm sure everything will be fine,' he said, maintaining a calm in his voice and reaching for his radio. 'Hello, control … Over.'

There was no response from the shortwave radio.

Samuel the guard had an automatic calmness about him, his background training had conditioned him for all sorts of situations and he was trying now to pacify the client by keeping a steady tone of voice. 'I'm sure the situation will be resolved soon,' adding, 'control will send someone down so it's best we hang on.'

It had now become apparent there was nothing they could do but wait.

Several minutes passed in silence.

Eventually Mr Goldstine spoke; there was less tension in his voice. 'I've been coming here for years and we have never spoken.'

Samuel nodded to acknowledge him.

'How long have you worked here?' asked Goldstine.

Samuel straightened with pride. 'Fifteen years, Sir.'

'That's an impressive record, you must feel pretty secure in the job. Excuse the pun.' his voice lightened.

'Yes, fifteen years and tomorrow is my last day, *I'm* retiring.'

'Are you looking forward to it?' Goldstine inquired.

'Yes and no … it's a bit of an unknown,' answered Samuel.

'Are you married?'

'Yes, with two grown up daughters: one now a

teacher, the other a doctor and married.' Samuel replied, adding the extra information to keep the conversation, going hoping to normalize the atmosphere.

'How long have you been married?' Goldstine still questioning.

'Thirty-nine years, by this September it will be our fortieth wedding anniversary,' said Samuel.

Goldstine responding with an assertive tone, 'Well, *I* beat you there, my wife and I have been married now sixty years this year. I think that's quite a record in this day and age, don't you?'

'Yes, that certainly is.' Samuel concurred, with a smile, feeling happier that the conversation had become calmer.

Goldstine continued to elaborate, '*I* also have two sons, plus grandchildren, and soon to become a great grandfather,' elaborating further, 'My sons are both in business, but I'm afraid with an easy upbringing they have not inherited my acumen for making money.' His voice expressed disappointment. Goldstine eased himself up half sitting on the stainless-steel table top. 'What line of business were you in before you became a security guard?'

'I served in the British armed forces for twenty-five years; I made the Army my career. Travelled around quite a bit, I've only had the two jobs more or less,' said Samuel, then realizing he may be revealing too much personal information, decided not to disclose he had served in the S.A.S.

'Did you see much action during that time?' Goldstine probing.

'Yes, Northern Ireland, Bosnia, and the Gulf as well as other operations,' said Samuel in a subtle tone.

'In a funny way we have been in the same line of business,' Goldstine stated nonchalantly.

'How do you mean?' said Samuel. with a quizzical expression in his voice.

'Well, you've used armaments during your career and my business has been supplying them.'

'You're an arms dealer?' Samuel concluded, his expression becoming serious, but trying not show his contempt.

'That's correct, been in the business some fifty odd years.'

Samuel looked at Goldstine's physique, thinking, God I bet this man has never been fit enough to have done anything active, let alone served in any armed forces. Yet here's a man capable of such devastating destruction, who has been indirectly responsible for a multitude of injury, death and displacement of life. It was a struggle for Samuel to be civil to a man of such wealth gained from others suffering.

Silence.

Samuel contemplated how to respond, then he felt compelled to say: 'Excuse my asking but don't you ever think of all the carnage caused by the armaments, due to your business?' Trying hard to be careful choosing his words.

'In other words, you're asking, do I have a conscience?' Goldstine stood up facing Samuel. Taking a conscious breath, then exhaling slowly, he placed both hands griping the edge of the table. Speaking in a decisive tone he continued. 'You sound like my sons. They keep going on about the ethics of what I do, but they never complain about their lifestyle, or what they will end up inheriting.' His voice now become slightly irate.

'I came to this country as a penniless child, a refugee from Holland just before the German occupation in 1940. I've worked hard for everything I've achieved. I suppose you're thinking why go into selling arms? Well, look at it this way, if I don't sell armaments to these people, someone else will step right up and sell them theirs. It's an open market; it's as simple as that. There's always someone else. Conscience!' he pondered, feeling he didn't have to justify what he had done, followed by saying: 'Where there is conflict, there is always the business. Conscience? No!'

Time was drifting on; still no sign of release.

By this time Goldstine had sat himself down on the chair behind the stainless-steel worktop, facing towards the vault door. He broke the silence, feeling the atmosphere and feeling obliged to change the subject.

'Anyway, being as it will be our Diamond Wedding anniversary next month, celebrating sixty years of marriage, I'm having a special present made for my wife. I had planned to go straight from here to the jewellery designer's this afternoon. I'm having them make a bespoke matching set of diamond jewellery with these stones.' Touching his flattened hand to his left chest pocket.

'Lucky lady, I'm sure it will be a nice surprise for her,' said Samuel, as the tone of the conversation lightened.

'Would you like to see them'? said Goldstine in a covetous tone.

'Yes, that would be interesting, I've never seen diamonds up close, only in jeweller's windows.'

Goldstine proceeded to take a small black velvet bag from his inside coat pocket, then pulling it gingerly open, proceeded to tip its contents into the palm of his hand. There! Eye dazzling lay five beautifully cut diamonds sparkling in the light.

'Wow! Your wife will be truly delighted.' Samuel remarked, with honest surprise.

'Yes, I hope so.' replied Goldstine. 'S*he* has no idea what I keep in my treasure trove. There's a small fortune in that collection.' He was now becoming more open, almost boastful. 'Sometimes I do a bit of business where the deal is done with merchandise instead of money. If you know what I mean,' He tapped the side of his nose.

Samuel did not comment.

Goldstine tipped the diamonds back into the small velvet bag, pulling the drawstring closed and replaced the little pouch into his inner coat pocket.

Just then the radio crackled. 'Hello, unit five are

you there? Over.'

'Yes, Unit five here. Over.'

'Hi, we seemed to have had a breakdown in communication, are you all right? Over.'

'Yes, we're fine. What's the situation? Over.'

'We have an ongoing incident. It involves two gunmen in the bank foyer although we have managed to stop it escalating by isolating the rest of the building. There is a possible hostage situation and a stand-off with the police, so the surrounding area of the bank is in lockdown. We are informed at present that the situation has been neutralized. Over.'

'When do you think it will be okay for the vault door be opened? Over'

'Hopefully the police can sort the situation as soon as poss, but in the meantime, it's advisable for you to stay put and wait for the all clear from the police. Over.'

'OK, we won't be going anywhere. Over' Samuel chuckled, turning to Goldstine. 'Sir, no doubt you caught all that about the armed men and the standoff with the police so we will just have to hang on until it's sorted.'

After hearing that, Goldstine became more resigned to their situation. 'Well, we certainty couldn't be in a safer place, even though it's damned inconvenient.' he retorted.

Yes, it's marvellous how these people get hold of their firearms. Samuel, would have liked to have commented, but instead said: 'Well, let's hope it gets resolved soon.'

'Thank God for that!' Goldstine physically showing relief by moving in the chair, relaxing and sitting back, trying to make himself more comfortable.

'Have you got any plans for your own anniversary.' Goldstine inquired.

'Well, I'm sure we will arrange something, a party of sorts, no doubt,' Samuel replied. 'I'll just have to see how my retirement finances work out.' Following on in a less hopeful tone. 'I've always wished I would be able one day to take my wife on a holiday to South Africa. Go back and visit my birth place and some of my relatives, so who knows,' with a shrug.

'South Africa; I've been there a few times in my line of work, it's certainly a lovely country.' said Goldstine, in a reminiscent mood. He slumped back in the chair. 'I'm whacked, going to shut my eyes for a bit, all this has just taken it out of me.' With that he lowered his head. The guard could see the situation had taken its toll on this aging man, so it was understandable he was tired.

Samuel decided to walk around the vault to stretch his legs. He felt good that Goldstine had wanted to rest, stop talking and let the atmosphere calm.

The vault was a good size space, the walls lined with banks of stainless-steel compartments. He felt it was amazing looking at all those rows and rows of little locked doors, all no doubt holding untold secrets, documents, monies, and of course jewellery. He knew it would be impossible to ever try to comprehend the wealth behind those locks, shaking his head in reckoning. As Goldstine had said what he had in his little box was his secret.

Samuel reminisced of his own past working life - had it all been worth it?

He had enjoyed working for the bank. It had been good for his mental health as he was sure he had suffered some form of P.T.S.D. Civilian life had enabled him to wind down and come to terms with the unforgettable scenes he had witnessed. The fact remained that, although he was proud of his service record and that he'd been able to serve his adopted country, he still pondered his position now he was retiring, and wondered had he really got the rewards he felt he deserved.

The time drifted on.

Samuel looked at his watch and immediately spoke into the short-wave radio. 'Unit five to control, unit five to control … do you read me? Over.'

'Control to unit five copy. Over.'

'What is the situation *now*? Over.' said Samuel with irritation in his tone.

'Unit five, we still have no clearance. Sorry, there's nothing we can do. Over.'

'Control, the security time lock will be activated shortly. Over.'

'Unit five, do you have the code to exit? Over.'

'Yes, we don't want to be here all night. Over.'

'Oh, hold on …. Unit five – good news. It seems things have improved. We have just heard that the two gunmen have been apprehended. We should have you out of there, hopefully, as soon as the police do a full reconnaissance of the premises and give the all clear. Over.'

Samuel was sitting on the edge of the other side of the worktop with his back towards Goldstine. He glanced at his watch, aware that it was 6.30pm, and knowing the security safe mechanism would activate the lock at 1900 hrs. But even though they would be able to exit from within the vault, he felt they did not want to get to that situation.

He looked over at Goldstine, still fast asleep. Standing slowly, he stretched himself from his seated position, then straightened his stature and, checking his attire, walked the few paces towards the vault door.

Just then the radio broke the silence. 'Hello, control to Unit five. Over.'

'Unit five, any news? Over.'

'Yes, we have been given the all clear, someone will be down to open up in about ten minutes. Over.'

'OK, great. Over and out.'

Samuel walked over towards Goldstine to rouse him, noticing the man had slumped even further down in the chair. Suddenly alarmed, he hastened beside him and, fearing the worst, checked his pulse. There was no sign. His first reaction was to get him down on to the floor to try and resuscitate him. No, first he must notify control to get medical aid.

'Unit five to control, we have an emergency, medical assistance paramedic required. Over.' He said urgently.

'Control to unit five, copy we are on our way,' They didn't even ask for an explanation.

Samuel had now managed to get Goldstine lying on his back on the floor and proceeded to place his hands on his chest. But the bulge in Goldstine's inner jacket pocket would obstruct and hamper the procedure. Samuel opened the jacket to one side to expose the man's shirted chest and then loosened his neck tie. Samuel was up to date with the practice of CPR, which had been part of the bank's in-house training, and he did his best. But even his best efforts were to no avail. By the time the paramedics came it was too late. They made a point of telling Samuel he had done a good job, but that there was nothing he could have done to help the old man's condition.

Samuel sat with his wife, Jo, seated on the veranda of the five-star hotel in Cape Town; they were enjoying watching the sun go down, with its glow reflecting over Table Mountain. They were celebrating their wedding anniversary for which Samuel had arranged a holiday to South Africa, something they had both dreamed of and looked forward to, but never thought it would become reality.

During their vacation they were able to visit relatives they had not seen for quite some time. It had also given them a chance to tour around, exploring the wild life reserves, and wonderful beaches. They had also been to see the Diamond Mining Museum; its exhibits showed how the diamonds were mined and included displays depicting the working condition of the miners and how they were strip searched at the end of their shift. Samuel remembered his father, who had worked in the mines, telling of how degrading it had been lined up in front of the white guards. In those days of apartheid, the workers were housed in compounds and were only allowed home occasionally. Although conditions have improved since those days, the Negro workers in the early days of mining were treated like slaves, living an appalling existence while the Dutch Diamond dynasties prospered in untold wealth.

Samuel had wondered how people like Goldstine had capitalized on these riches. How his armaments had furnished militant groups and other terrorist organizations throughout the world, with equipment through his back door deals. Samuel had himself borne witness to the atrocities of conflict, fuelled by the power of such weaponry.

Sitting in the warm evening watching the sunset, Samuel concluded that they deserved a little bit of luxury after their hard-working lives. He held Jo's hand, watching the light as it caught the large diamond set in the ring on her finger: his anniversary present to her. He had told her how much he wished the stone was the real thing. But Jo just loved it '*It's so gorgeous all the same.*' she had said. Samuel just smiled to himself. If she had known its real value, she would be too scared to wear it.

Did he have a conscience?

No!

The Rolling Hills of Wiltshire

I have been to northern places
Where the mountains touch the sky
I've walked the glens and crags
And watch the eagles fly so high
But my heart still calls me back
To where it holds the key

Chorus

In the rolling hills of Wiltshire
That where I love to be
In the rolling hills of Wiltshire
The place that's home to me

I have seen across the lakes and vales
To deep valleys full of trees
Looked down from the tallest beacons
To rivers flowing to the seas
But my spirit's like a homing bird
And knows where it should be

Chorus

As I've toured around great cities
Shipping ports and industry
Through crowded streets with towering building
But that is no place for me
And as I've travelled many roads
My inner soul just longs to be

Chorus

Of all the wonders of this land
I've stood in awe of its scenery
And all these places that I've been
In this our great country
For there's one view I'll never tire
And my eyes can't wait to see, It's

Chorus

In the rolling hills of Wiltshire
That's where I love to be
In the rolling hills of Wiltshire
The place that's home to me

In the rolling hills of Wiltshire
Is the place that's home to me-e

The Bond

They sat together in the autumn park. Bob's eyes watched the leaves falling from the trees following their rocking motion on the breeze before landing on the grass. Sam relaxed sitting next to him on the bench, retaining his skateboard under one foot, his attention drawn to a couple of girls who had just walked past; he was now of that age. Sam was just over three years older than Bob, another difference between them. Although they lived together as part of the same family, Bob was adopted.

In spite of these differences, they had grown up treating each other like siblings. Bob took comfort in the way his life had turned out.

Bob could remember the time when Sam's parents first came to the home. They had spoken to the lady in charge, then talked to Bob directly. Although he didn't understand what they were saying, their tone seemed very nice and they had kind faces. Sometime later they came again, this time bringing Sam with them. Bob also remembered all of them going into a room with a desk and hearing them talk for a while. The atmosphere had been happy, he had sensed that Sam's parents were excited. Afterwards they had shaken hands with the lady and then Sam's mother had picked Bob up and taken him with them.

Outside Sam's father had opened the car's rear door; once Sam was in, he had sat Bob next to him on the back seat. It had felt exciting going along in the car.

In a short while they had arrived at their home and unloaded the car. Indoors, Bob had sat on the floor next to Sam. They had been a little shy of each other at first but after a short while had accepted each other's company. Eventually, Sam's Dad had let them both share the same bedroom and in no time they had become inseparable, both getting up to all sorts of pranks. Sam sometimes let Bob take the blame when they made a mess but for these boys it was all great fun.

Over time, Sam's Mum and Dad would take them to all sorts of places, all gelling as a family. Bob couldn't remember his own parents or the home life he'd come from, everything was a blank in a distant past. Both boys just loved being out in the fresh air and it wasn't long before they were running about under their own steam. Bob challenged Sam as they got older, realizing that he was able to outrun, and catch a ball better than him.

By now Sam was into books and studying and off at school at which he excelled, always looking smart in his uniform. Bob was unable to compete with that and Sam's parents knew his limitations. Irrespective of the difference in their abilities, they still got on really well; you could call it brotherly love, a bond that didn't require words.

Gradually, Sam got into sport at school, so it was more fun him being active for both of them to enjoy time together. Sam even made the local under-sixteens football club. Sunday mornings were spent at the edge of the pitch, Bob with Sam's Dad watching the game. He could tell his Dad was proud as he shouted Sam's name when he had the ball.

By now Sam was able run fast so it became a real challenge for Bob to keep up, plus now Sam was really good with his skateboard. It fascinated Bob to watch him perform his tricks at the skateboard park.

Here they were the two of them, Saturday morning in the park having some time out together.

"Better get home for lunch now," said Sam. Bob turned and looked at him. He stood up; he knew what to do.

"Race you to the gates," shouted Sam as he jumped onto his skateboard, shooting off down the path with Bob in hot pursuit now having a job to keep up as his energy levels waned. He had started to feel it lately, it was part of his metabolism. Sam was at the gates before him.

"Come on, slow coach!" laughed Sam.

Bob was panting as they walked through the gates to the edge of the pavement; the road was busy. Sam put his hand into his pocket, then bent down towards him.

"Better put this on." He said, as he held Bob's collar to clip on the lead, then stroking his head. "Come on Bobby, old boy." Said Sam as they crossed the road towards home.

Trees

Trees our natural history,
hold part of the scenery
These living structures,
defined so individually
They stand their ground,
against winds and drought
Some casting their leaves
when the year is out
Their life needs like us,
nourished by rain and sun
But against chainsaws,
their power to resist is done
The needs of man are great,
wood must be the harvest
Manufacturing, construction,
this consumption has no rest
Taking habitat away from one life,
to furnish another
As man fights for planet space,
consumes its earth mother
To clear a space for crops to grow,
and cattle roam
We breed and multiply,
expand as if alone, must have a home
This way of man's lifestyle,
has to slow, compromise at last
It's not too late to take back
these plunderers' ways of greed, to task
Now try, replace the years
already spent with devastation
Try and repair the damage

done to this vast deforestation
Planting saplings has begun,
to show willing, a possibility
So, think of the future,
take up the spade go plant a tree
Leave A Legacy
Make shade for our children's children
to behold, that you will never see.

Star Of Bethlehem

Melody request from lesfleur2@hotmail.co.uk

There's a light There's a light
Shining in the sky
It's the star of Bethlehem
A guiding light to show the way
For the travelling three wise men

There's a light There's a light
Shining in the sky
A host of angels sing glory be
Proclaiming Jesus in a stable born
Calling shepherds to come and
see

There's a light There's a light
Shining in the sky
We must be strong in this
world we live
All the turmoil now we see
and hear
With its conflict, it's hard to
forgive

There's a light There's a light
Shining in the sky
Showing Christ was born to save
So take this hand that's offered you
From your birth, until the grave

There's a light There's a light
Shining in the sky
Just let yourself therefore believe
Then you will know it's really true
From the comfort you will receive

There's a light There's a light
Shining in the sky
See it shine out across the sea
Offering peace and hope to all mankind
Around the world, for all eternity

Wishing you all a Happy Christmas

Christmas day enjoy the act of giving
That gift of time to one another
Magical moments a life to cherish
Seek reason with a faith renewed
Keep hold the dreams of possibilities
Hope for peace in this world of trouble
So whatever you do don't burst the bubble

Taken from an original watercolour
by the late Peter Ward
As a Tribute to an Artist and Friend

Why?

(Young Solder at the Winter Front Line)

Why have I been conscripted
Why am I wearing this uniform in the army
Why do I need to carry a gun to do my duty
Why am I far from home in someone else's country
Why am I to fight the enemy when we are the
invaders
Why did I write the letter, that I wouldn't send
Why must I kill other people's brothers, son, or
husbands

Why is that explosion so! I'm moving fast through to
air
Why have I a burning pain in my back, and lying in
the snow
Why has everything gone so quiet, I can't hear myself
shouting
Why is the snow all around me becoming stained red
Why is it I can no longer feel my body
Why is it I feel so sleepy, and just want to close my
eyes.

Memories: Some gems are yours and yours alone

Memories are ours to have and to hold
Through childhood to our later years
The mind absorbs our uncharted way
This rich pattern helps guide happiness or fears

Gathered from our life's journey
Some from love, joy, warmth and care
Others in denial, best forgotten
Or conjure sorrow, hatred, and despair

A colour or smell that jars the mind
Oh, to reminisce when you hear that tune
That taste of a holiday long gone
Or under the stars looking up at the moon

Sometimes they bring a smile
A personal pleasure, a twinkle to the eye
For reasons you can't describe
Evoke feelings with a warm comforting sigh

Parties, family gatherings flood the mind
Time made memories for others to share
Remembrance of the brave lives given
Or someone dear no longer there

Ponder of the special time
One fonder that rises above the rest
A love so young and so sublime
Of passion spent of tender heart caressed

Some memories are always there
Many linger for only you alone to care
Emotions flowing back, why so unfair
Not to be shared, but only yours to bear

Comes later life as the years roll by
In old age you talk referring to the past
Recall all those memories held dear
Realising now, your life has been too fast

Time will come when you are no longer here
You maybe someone else's memory, held dear

Here we are again
Is it really true
A full twelve months to play with
What are you going to do?

Postface

I have always loved music of all types. One of the things I would have liked to have done during my life is write songs for a living. Metaphorically speaking this book is my LP ... so I hope you at least like one of the tracks.

Acknowledgements

I would like to thank everyone who has been involved in helping bring this book to fruition. These people have given their time to help inspire, coach, advise, nurture, proof read, edit and finally format ready to self-publish.

Particularly, Joy Simon who gave generous permission for me to reproduce eight of her female portraits

I have been very fortunate to have my partner's input and comments, and also in having personal friends whom have read and helped correct spelling, grammar, and punctuation. Not forgetting the writing groups with which I have been involved, to prompt, inspire, help and encourage me.

June White who prompted me to write. Iris Lerpiniere for reading and valued critique. George Liddell (Creative Writing), Greg Atkins and Christina Sanders (Writing Space) for their help and guidance. Peter and Jenny Ward for their enthusiasm, reading and helping with my grammar and spelling. Robert Cook improving my computer skills (Community at 67). Jennifer Kendrick for her reading, suggestions and introduction. Not forgetting Patricia Main, whose efforts in bringing this collection of work together, by editing, collating and formatting, have made it ready to be published.

About the Editor:

Patricia Main began life in London's East End in an era before it became fashionable and has an enduring love for the City (especially in its Early Modern manifestation) despite spending most of her life in the South West of England. When not researching history for publication or editing texts written by others, she writes a variety of fiction.

You can find her on Facebook – **Patricia Ainger – Writer**. She also has a website (very much a work in progress) – **www.patricia.ainger.com** and loves to hear from readers.